The Oregon Escort

Susan Page Davis

Heartsong Presents

To my dear husband, Jim, the perfect husband for me; the
patient and loving father of my children; my first editor and
best friend.

A note from the Author:
*I love to hear from my readers! You may correspond with
me by writing:*

**Susan Page Davis
Author Relations
PO Box 721
Uhrichsville, OH 44683**

ISBN 1-59310-949-0

THE OREGON ESCORT

All scripture quotations are taken from the King James Version of the
Bible.

All of the characters and events in this book are fictitious. Any resem-
blance to actual persons, living or dead, or to actual events is purely
coincidental.

*Our mission is to publish and distribute inspirational products offering
exceptional value and biblical encouragement to the masses.*

PRINTED IN THE U.S.A.

Another cascade of arrows whistled into the cavern, and Mike knew he had to stop them.

He had pinpointed the location of the warrior with the rifle behind a gnarled clump of brush. He wasn't so sure about the other two. He'd hoped at least one was out of the action, but from the intense fire, there had to be three of them left.

Doggedly, he watched the spot from which the gunfire had come, praying for a clear shot. It was close enough, but he couldn't just blaze away at them. His supply of lead and powder cartridges was nearly gone, and he wasn't known as a sharpshooter. Every bullet had to count.

He saw movement to his left and turned, knowing it was too late if the aim was true.

SUSAN PAGE DAVIS and her husband, Jim, have been married thirty years and have six children, ages eleven to twenty-eight. They live in Maine, where they are active in an independent Baptist church. Susan is a homeschooling mother and news writer. She has published short stories in the romance, humor, and mystery fields. This is her second published novel, and she would love to hear from readers.

Books by Susan Page Davis

HEARTSONG PRESENTS
HP607—Protecting Amy

one

"No, sir, I can't take you." The corporal's slight Southern accent made his words soft and apologetic, but Lydia Jackson could tell from the steel in the set of his jaw that he would not change his mind.

She stood in the shadow of the Gordon family's covered wagon, where it sat outside Fort Laramie in the hot July sun. She had spent the first half of 1860 getting this far, and the cavalryman examining the Gordons' team of mules seemed determined to delay their progress.

"But, Corporal, we have to go," Mr. Gordon protested.

The trooper bent to lift one of the nearest mule's hooves and looked at it, then put it down gently and stood. "Sorry. These animals won't make it to Independence Rock."

Mrs. Gordon stepped forward, her eyes blazing. "Who gives you the right to make that decision? We've come all the way from Pennsylvania with these mules."

Corporal Brown frowned and shook his head. "They're on their last legs, ma'am. Maybe you can trade them for another team or stay here at Fort Laramie for a month or so and rest them."

When the corporal left the Gordons and headed toward the next wagon, Lydia hurried after him.

"Corporal."

He swung around and met her gaze, and she halted in her tracks. His worn uniform suited him perfectly, with the high-topped black boots, blue jacket with brass buttons, and lighter blue trousers with gold stripes down the sides. Like many troopers, he had abandoned the army-issue forage cap in favor of a wide-brimmed, soft felt hat, and the cavalry's crossed saber insignia was pinned to the crown. He pulled it off, revealing thick, brown hair tumbling across his brow.

"Yes, miss?"

Regardless of his dashing uniform, the corporal's most striking feature was his rich brown eyes. They took in her every move as she stepped closer. Lydia made herself break the stare first. There was something about the way he watched her that made her heart race.

"Pardon me," she began, feeling a flush creep up from the high neck of her dress. "I've been traveling with the Gordons since Missouri. Did I understand correctly that you're refusing to let them continue with the wagon train?"

"Yes, miss. I have strict orders from Sergeant Reese. No wagons without fit teams will proceed."

Lydia inhaled deeply. The Gordons' team was lean and footsore, but they'd held out this long. That meant they were tough, didn't it?

"I must get to Oregon City by fall." She lowered her gaze, embarrassed that she had voiced her thought. It was none of his concern.

But the corporal's sudden, empathetic smile sent a thrill through her. "Best be making other arrangements, then, miss. There's a family yonder with two wagons and a passel of children. I expect they could use a hand."

Lydia knew he was referring to the Sawyers, and she refused to consider them. Mr. Sawyer whipped his mules and yelled at his children. But there were other, more peaceful families she could ask.

"You're certain about the Gordons?"

"Yes, miss, they'd be risking their lives to go on with those mules. But they can wait here a few weeks for another train."

Lydia nodded. She hated to see the Gordons turned out of the wagon train, but the officers leading the cavalry unit that would accompany them from Fort Laramie to Oregon had the final say.

"I hope you find a place in the train, miss," he said softly, and Lydia gulped. It would be brassy to reply to such a forward remark. Wouldn't it? She felt her face go scarlet.

"Thank you," she managed to get out, and he smiled again. It wasn't a leering, offensive smile. It was more of an encouraging, friendly smile, she decided as she hurried across the trampled grass toward the Gordons' wagon.

≈

Mike Brown stood watching the young woman as she glided away into the dusk. Seldom did one encounter such a pretty sight on the plains of Wyoming. He wondered what she was doing out here, traveling alone. Her refined speech and high-quality clothing told him she was accustomed to an easier life than he'd known. New England, he guessed from her inflection. Her hair, pinned up on her head, caught the last rays of sunlight and gleamed auburn. She had been months on the trail, yet she walked erect and with grace. And those blue eyes. . .

He took a slow, careful breath and turned away. He had no business looking over the women of the wagon train. Sergeant Reese had reminded him just this morning that they would have to keep an eye on the thirty troopers in their escort detail.

"Can't let the men form attachments with the civilian girls," Reese had said. "It makes for trouble later on."

Mike had agreed with him at the time. But that was before a young woman with the bearing and complexion of a princess had come to talk with him. He realized he hadn't thought about a woman this way in a long, long time. He wasn't sure he liked it.

≈

Lydia went to the back of the wagon and climbed over the tailboard. She'd been with the Gordons for nearly two months. She'd offered her services of cooking, doing laundry, and watching the children in exchange for a niche in the wagon for her belongings and the protection of the family. Mr. and Mrs. Gordon were not warm or sentimental, but they had befriended her in their aloof way, and she had come to care about twelve-year-old John Paul and the three little girls. However, she would not stop a month at Fort Laramie while their overworked mules recovered.

She rooted her belongings from the tightly packed wagon. The three Gordon girls watched her, their faces sad and their eyes wide.

"I've got to leave you," Lydia told them. "Be good, now. I'll miss you." The youngest, Clara, began to cry, and Lydia gathered them to her in a brief embrace. Then she heaved her carpetbag down and climbed out to lift down her small, leather-bound trunk of books. Mrs. Gordon walked toward her, shoulders sagging.

"What are you doing, Lydia?"

"I need to find a berth in the train, Mrs. Gordon. I'm sorry, but if you're staying here, I'll have to part from you."

"No, please. You can stay with us. You've no one to go to."

Lydia shrugged. "You've been very kind, but I need to go on."

"I don't know if I can get along without you. You've been so good with the children!"

"And I'll miss them, but you'll be fine. A few weeks' rest here will do you good."

Mrs. Gordon sighed. "You helped buy supplies for the next part of the journey."

Lydia swallowed. She couldn't afford to lose that.

"Let me speak to my husband," Mrs. Gordon said wearily.

"Thank you." Lydia set her bags to one side. "I should try to make arrangements immediately. The wagons will pull out at first light."

Mrs. Gordon nodded. "You go see about transportation, and I'll pack you up some flour, beans, and bacon."

Lydia headed toward the Paines' wagon. They were one of a dozen families that had come out together from Independence. The rest had been waiting at the fort until the army decreed the party large enough to warrant an escort. Lydia didn't know them well, but she perceived Mr. Paine as a quiet man who cared well for his oxen. His wife, Dorcas, had a good heart and a sweet, cheerful face. Their two children were lively but clean and obedient. Yes, the Paines were Lydia's first choice.

The sun was down, and she felt insecure and alone. The wagon camp sprawled across the meadow near the fort, and an Indian encampment lay nearby.

"Can we help you, ma'am?" Two troopers appeared out of the dusk, and Lydia shrank from them with distrust. The addition of the troopers to the party aroused mixed feelings in her heart. She ought to feel more secure with an official escort, but the men seemed altogether too eager to socialize.

"No, thank you." She hurried on.

Mrs. Paine was drying the supper dishes, and her husband sat silently beside the fire with a drowsy little girl on his knee. The eight-year-old boy was sprawled on a blanket near the back wagon wheel, staring up at the sky.

"Excuse me." Lydia entered the circle of flickering light.

Mr. Paine stirred as if he would rise but sank back with two-year-old Jenny in his arms, giving Lydia a nod. His wife's greeting was more effusive.

"Well, good evening, Miss Jackson! My dear, isn't this exciting? We shall be off at dawn with a large company, and thirty strapping soldiers to protect us."

Lydia smiled. "Yes, ma'am. I was—"

"They're even sending a doctor along." Mrs. Paine smiled as she lifted the basin of dirty dishwater. "We have it so much better than those who traveled this road in the past."

"Yes, ma'am. I—"

"Although Mr. Miller has done a fine job as wagon master. I'm certain we could have made it on our own, but it's comforting to know we won't have to."

"Indeed," Lydia said with a gulp. Would she ever get to make her request?

The stolid man by the fire came to her rescue.

"Mrs. Paine," he said quietly, "I believe Miss Jackson came on an errand."

"Oh." His wife stopped with the tin basin swung back, ready to toss out the tepid water, and stared at Lydia in the dimness. "Forgive me, my dear. What is it?"

Lydia smiled. Dorcas Paine was perhaps ten years her senior, and she was quite pretty, with her blond hair bound in a crocheted snood. She had been a bit on the plump side when they left Independence, but Lydia could see she had lost some weight and was looking healthy and still a bit rounded. Her enthusiastic kindness appealed to everyone, and she enjoyed conversing with nearly anyone, at any time.

"I find myself in somewhat of a bind," Lydia began, glancing from Dorcas to her husband. Mr. Paine appeared to be nodding off, his hair dark against little Jenny's blond curls.

"In what way?" Dorcas asked.

"I need to change my travel arrangements."

Dorcas swung the basin, and the water shot out with a neat *plop* onto the scrubby grass. "You're leaving the Gordons."

Lydia nodded. "The troopers told them they must rest their team if they can't replace them. I felt it best to find another situation."

"Quite right." Dorcas hung the basin on a nail in the side of the wagon box. "I've seen you with the children. You've been a good helper to Mrs. Gordon."

"Thank you." Lydia waited, anxiety creeping over her. It was getting late. She wanted the matter settled.

"I'm sure any family in this train would be pleased to accommodate you," Dorcas said.

"I have a few supplies," Lydia murmured, trying not to let her desperation show.

Dorcas nodded. "I shall speak to Mr. Paine."

Lydia swallowed hard, wondering when that would be. Mr. Paine appeared to be asleep, slouching lower by the minute. But he raised his head at that moment and said clearly, "As you wish, Mrs. Paine." He stood slowly, his little daughter in his arms, and headed for the back of the wagon.

Before Lydia could speak, Dorcas clapped her hands. "There! You see? It's settled."

"Are you certain?"

"Of course, my dear. What Mr. Paine says is so, is so. He's

very pleased you're joining us."

Lydia returned Dorcas's smile, wondering how one determined that Mr. Paine was pleased.

"Thank you. I can't tell you how relieved I am. I'll help you in any way I can."

"It will be delightful. Why don't you fetch your things now? It will be simpler in the morning if you're right here. You must be used to sleeping on the ground?"

"Oh, yes," Lydia assured her.

"Well, then, I shan't worry about your discomfort, since there's no changing that. We shall have a splendid time together."

Mr. Paine had laid Jenny down to sleep and was stooping over the boy as Lydia walked past.

"Come, Nathan," he said softly. "Let's get your shoes off."

Lydia compared his quiet, solid presence and his gentle way with his children to Mr. Gordon's brusque manner. When Mr. Gordon was around, his whole family was on edge, knowing a reprimand was only a breath away.

She hurried toward the Gordons' wagon, striding more confidently. Things would be better from here on. Dorcas Paine seemed delighted at the change, making the remainder of the harsh trip sound like the most pleasant outing imaginable. Lydia was determined to do her part, helping with the chores and watching the children.

The Gordons' wagon was not where she left it, but John Paul was stretched out on the turf beside Lydia's luggage.

"Where did your parents go?" She tried to keep the anxiety from her voice as she reached for her carpetbag.

John Paul sat up and yawned. "Pa took the wagon closer to the fort so the army will think he's staying."

Lydia stopped with her hand in midair. "What do you mean?"

The boy smirked. "We'll wait an hour or so after the wagons leave; then we'll follow them."

Lydia stared at him in disbelief. "But Corporal Brown says he won't take you unless you have a different team."

"Pa says if we catch up the next day, they can't send us back."

Lydia picked up her large bag. If the Gordons wanted to strike out on their own after the wagons left and hoped to catch up with the train, no one could stop them. But what if the corporal was right? What if they got a score of miles from the fort and the mules went lame? She shuddered to think of the family's fate alone in the wilderness.

She reached for her small workbag. A gunnysack lay on the grass. "What's that?"

"That's your food. Ma says if you want to stay with us, you're welcome. If not, that goes with you."

Lydia hoisted the sack to test its weight. It couldn't hold nearly enough food for an adult for the arduous trip ahead. She had given Mr. Gordon the money for her share of the food back in Independence. She considered marching up to him and demanding a larger share of provisions. John Paul was watching her, and she took a deep breath.

"I'm going with the Paines. Can you carry that little trunk to their wagon for me?"

"You're taking all your books," he said wistfully.

"Well, of course."

John Paul lifted the trunk to his shoulder and nodded toward the burlap sack. "Hope you didn't want any coffee."

two

Lydia trudged along beside the wagon. They were only two days out of Fort Laramie, but already she had abandoned all hope of returning to the civilized world. A shack of a house stood near the ferry this morning, but they hadn't met a soul or passed a dwelling since.

Twenty dusty, sun-baked miles from the fort, her lips were cracked, her skin was dry, and her eyes smarted from the alkali dust that swirled in the constant wind. Her purpose had shriveled and shrunk to the basic need of putting this mile behind her.

The wind whipped her skirt around her legs, tripping her up repeatedly. She stumbled and pulled the layers of cloth free, then went on. She could ride in the wagon if she wanted, but she wouldn't do that until she was exhausted.

Back in Nebraska, she had tried riding in the wagon, but she hated sitting there while the animals strained to pull her weight across the interminable prairie. She trudged on, telling herself that she was moving herself closer to her goal and not causing more work for the Paines' oxen.

"I've walked over a thousand miles." Unthinkable a year ago, but now it was just a fact, like the layer of chalky dust that dulled her auburn hair and her grimy cotton dress. Already the two-week stop at Fort Laramie, while the smaller wagon trains reformed into this large one, seemed a hazy dream.

The wind gusted again and caught her skirt, billowing it out in front of her. Lydia gasped and turned into the blast in hopes that would help, but the voluminous skirt and threadbare petticoat beneath it fought her for every inch of modesty.

Just when she was able to smooth the skirt down over her knees, another blast buffeted her, and she struggled once more with the flapping fabric.

A hearty laugh rang out, and she spun around, bending over to hold her skirt against her shins.

"You'd best hang on to something, miss, or you'll be scudding off like a schooner under full sail." The lanky young man was Trooper Barkley, a friendly fellow who was always ready to lend the pioneers a hand. He and another soldier were riding their horses alongside the wagons, and Lydia saw to her chagrin that his companion was the handsome Southerner, Corporal Brown.

"No," said Brown, "she'll just roll off like a tumbleweed in the breeze, until she fetches up in some ravine."

Barkley guffawed. "No offense, miss. Can we help you into your wagon?"

"No, thank you," Lydia said between clenched teeth, walking backward to keep up with the Paines' wagon and trying unsuccessfully to tame the full skirt. She avoided looking at the men but couldn't help snatching glances at Brown. His eyes glittered, and he didn't seem the least bit fatigued.

He was used to this life, she guessed, and he was riding a beautiful bay mare. Anyone would feel more alive riding a horse like that. She'd seen her earlier when her glossy hide gleamed in the morning sun. But now, like everything else, she was coated with dust. Her face had an appealing sweetness, but Lydia had seen the mare sidestep and throw her head, crow-hopping obstinately. She suspected Brown had his hands full for the first hour on the bay's back that morning. Now, after half a day under saddle, the mare walked docilely beside Barkley's dun gelding.

But it was the rider who drew her attention. Lydia found herself looking up at Brown again, and he smiled down at her. Those eyes! She had to quit staring, even if he didn't seem to mind.

"Here you go." Brown fished in his saddlebag and produced a small leather pouch. He stopped the mare and leaned down from the saddle, holding it out to her.

"What's this?"

"Lead shot. Stitch a row in the hem of your skirt."

"The idea!" Lydia shrank away from him, shocked that he would speak to her with such familiarity. Had she somehow betrayed in her glance the way her heart beat faster when he was around? The amusement in his eyes and Barkley's turned her embarrassment into anger. "Keep it! Put it to good use when we're attacked by savages."

"Better'n showing off your laces and linens," Brown replied with a shrug.

"Prettiest view I've seen in a long while," Barkley agreed.

She felt her face go scarlet as she pushed Brown's gloved hand away, but letting go of her uncooperative skirt proved near disastrous. It billowed up, again exposing her pantalets and petticoat.

"Easy, now, Matthew," Brown said to his companion with a touch of annoyance. "That's no way to address a lady."

"Sorry, miss." Barkley had the grace to look chastised.

She turned her back to them and the wind, pressing her skirt down against her thighs as she strode to catch up with the Paines' plodding wagon. She heard Barkley chuckle, and it infuriated her that the men found her situation diverting. She had considered Brown a gentleman, though now it appeared he was only one notch above the other men when it came to courtesy. They trotted past on their horses, and Brown tipped his hat.

"No offense intended, miss."

&

"Brown, two wagons are lagging behind. You and Gleason ride back and hurry them up. Don't want to get too big a gap between them and the rest of the train."

Brown threw his sergeant, Dan Reese, a curt salute and wheeled the mare. How could anything be lagging behind? That meant they were going slower than these overgrown tortoises!

In the two days they'd come from Fort Laramie, the emigrants had settled into the routine. Most were already seasoned travelers, having come from Missouri early in the summer as soon as the grass was high enough to sustain the cattle. They had walked clear across Nebraska beside their lumbering wagons. Brown was thankful that his job entailed riding a horse or a mule. At the moment it was a horse, and a good one at that. The showy bay mare fidgeted too much, wasting a lot of energy fighting the bit, but once she settled down, she was a good mount. Not one he would choose for a combat detail, but for this duty she was fine, with a more comfortable stride than one of the steadier mules would have.

Gleason joined him, and they trotted along the line of sixty creaking wagons.

"Not bad for summer duty, hey?" Gleason asked with a grin.

Brown nodded. "It beats hanging around the fort pulling fatigue details and drilling in the sun."

In some ways, escort duty was even better than chasing hostile Indians, although 99 percent of the time, that wasn't bad either. It was the 1 percent, when you found yourself a hapless target, that got uncomfortable. The escort service operated from early summer, when the first wagon trains reached Fort Laramie, to late fall, when the last train had been safely delivered to Oregon. For an enlisted man, this was perhaps the best job in the West.

It wasn't like staying at the fort as the emigrant trains passed through. The men traveled along with the same folks for several weeks, helping them and training them to survive the rigorous journey. One could get to know them, even make friends. For most of the men, it was a rare opportunity to socialize with decent women.

Like the girl who had joined the Paines at Fort Laramie. Feisty. A little standoffish. Brown wasn't sure why such a straitlaced girl would want to go west alone. Maybe she had a husband waiting out there. But she had nice clothes. They were becoming shabby, like those of all emigrants who had come this far, but he could see that her dusty dresses were made of good cloth and well cut, not to mention the deep lace flounces on her underthings. He smiled as he remembered her outrage when Matt Barkley intimated that he'd seen them. It wasn't polite to suggest that a lady had anything under her skirt. Pretty girl, though. Very pretty. And she had some backbone.

He noticed that he was nearly back to the Paines' place in line, but when he came even with their wagon, Lydia Jackson was nowhere in sight. Just as well. He and Gleason had a task before them. He urged the mare into a canter.

❧

After the wagons circled that evening, Lydia helped Dorcas prepare the meal and care for the children. Her spirits were still low, and every time she glimpsed a uniform, she turned her back hastily. She tried to pay attention to Mrs. Paine's incessant chatter, but her mind kept straying back to Corporal Brown's practical offer of his shot pouch.

Perhaps she should have taken it. But she was determined not to give any of the thirty troopers reason to think they could take liberties during the trip. Still, the winds were worse than ever, and she couldn't walk all day showing off her ankles and more. Brown was right about that.

She looked down at the ground, wondering if small pebbles might serve the same purpose as the lead.

"Evening, ma'am."

Lydia whirled to see Brown and Barkley approaching the fireside.

"Good evening, gentlemen," Dorcas cooed with a bright smile. The small, vivacious woman had room in her heart for all things motherless, and she looked on the troopers as boys who had been too long away from their families.

"We'd be happy to escort you to get water, ma'am," Barkley said, his glance sweeping over Lydia and back to Mrs. Paine. They had stopped for the night near a stream that was fairly clear before it flowed into the muddy Platte.

"That's very kind." Dorcas brushed her hands together. "We do need water. Lydia, dear, would you mind. . ."

Lydia fixed her gaze on Brown, who was watching her

with an enigmatic smile. She flushed, recalling his earlier impertinence. "Yes, I would mind, Mrs. Paine. I shan't go out of sight of the train with these men."

Dorcas blinked at her. "Really, dear, these are gentlemen." She threw a flustered glance toward Brown. "Take Nathan with you, then." The boy was setting out the tin plates and cups, but looked up when he heard his name.

"Several other ladies will be along," Brown said. "We're passing the word."

He seemed amused. Lydia refused to be embarrassed. She nodded curtly and walked toward the wagon, where two pails hung from the side board.

A few minutes later she, a dozen other women, and a few children walked to the stream behind Corporal Brown, carrying their buckets. Lydia hung back to avoid him and consequently found herself nearest Barkley, who was bringing up the rear and attempting to look very alert and efficient for the benefit of the three single women in the group.

"Wind's died down," he offered, and Lydia wondered if he were referring to the earlier incident. She decided he was merely making small talk.

"Does it ever quit altogether?" she asked.

"Not out here." He shifted his rifle into the crook of his arm and held a branch back for her. They had come down a steep bank into the flats beside the water, and a few willow trees grew there, with brambles scattered among them. Nathan ran ahead of her with the other children.

"Mike's right about the lead shot."

Lydia stopped short and stared at Barkley. "How dare you!"

Surprise heightened the private's eyebrows. "I beg your pardon, miss. We didn't mean to insult you. All the ladies who come out here learn to weight their skirts down, or else they take to wearing bloomers."

"Bloomers?" Lydia's outrage was mounting. "That's disgraceful!"

Barkley shook his head with such innocence that she wondered if she had misjudged him. "No offense intended, miss. I grew up near Fort Bridger, and we seen a lot of Mormon ladies come through. They all wear 'em."

Lydia eyed him doubtfully. "You don't say."

"I do say. Their church told 'em to. You can see why."

She stared at him. No, Barkley was not toying with her. Still, she had heard all sorts of outlandish tales about the Mormons.

"Is it true they walked all the way across these plains, pulling their things in carts?"

"Some of 'em. A lot of suffering before they got where they was gittin'."

"So your family lives out there?"

"My brother and his wife still do. My folks passed on."

She decided, to her chagrin, that Barkley knew what he was talking about. Perhaps she ought to listen to him and Brown, as much as it galled her.

"So. . .lead shot?"

Barkley grinned. "Yes, miss. Open a little gap in the hem and run a row of pellets in, then stitch it tight. My mother used to do it."

Lydia frowned at the thought of carrying a couple extra pounds around all the time, but that would be better than adopting a masculine costume like bloomers. Aunt Moriah would have been mortified to think her niece would wear the scandalous fashion.

"I don't suppose rocks would do?" she ventured.

"I'll get you some lead when we get back to the train." There was sympathy in Barley's voice now. "Lead's heavier than most rocks, and it hangs better when they're all the same size."

She nodded meekly.

"And I won't tell Mike I gave it to you."

Her rage surfaced once more at his implication that she cared what Corporal Brown thought. She pulled in a sharp breath. Her instinct was to set Barkley in his place with no question as to her feelings about him, Michael Brown, and the entire U.S. Army. But at that moment she wasn't sure what those feelings were.

"Thank you." She turned and strode quickly toward the stream bank.

Corporal Brown was standing at ease, looking back over the trail, his eyes scanning the landscape. Lydia tried not to look at him, but she couldn't resist one quick glance. He did make a dashing figure in his uniform, tall and clear-eyed. It was comforting to have a man as stalwart and alert as Brown keeping watch while they filled their buckets, she told herself, although his stubborn jaw was a bit annoying.

He glanced toward her then and smiled, and Lydia looked quickly away. Part of her wanted to smile back, but the other part didn't want to give him the satisfaction. Was he presumptuous, or was he simply a friendly person? It didn't matter. She had a purpose in life, and starting a flirtation with a cavalry trooper was not part of it. She called to Nathan and made sure she didn't come close enough for Brown to speak to her.

three

It was twilight when they got back to the camp. Brown and Barkley delivered each of the ladies to her campfire with a cheery good night, but when they came to the Paines' wagon, Lydia left their group without a word.

Mrs. Paine, however, was more gracious. "Thank you, gentlemen. It's a comfort to have you along."

Brown nodded and smiled at her. "Have a good evening, ma'am." He moved on with the others, wondering how long Lydia would be able to ignore him. She was a pleasure to look at, with her lovely face, thick, reddish-brown hair, and keen blue eyes, but it would be a long summer if she kept up her stiff refinement.

He reached for Mrs. Adams's bucket, now that they were within the safety of the camp and he didn't need to keep his gun at the ready. He was scheduled to stand watch for a couple of hours after midnight, but he always checked the detachment's livestock himself in the evening. The Sioux would love to pick up some extra animals if they had the chance.

As they left Mrs. Williams off, a stir sounded at the opening on the east side of the wagon corral, and Brown turned toward the noise.

"What is it?" Barkley asked, peering through the dimness. Several men were gathered near the gap they used as a gate each evening, between the lead wagon and the last.

Brown thrust the pail of water at him. "See Mrs. Adams to her wagon." He went quickly to the gathering, arriving on the heels of Sergeant Reese.

"What's going on?" Reese barked, pushing his way to the center of the knot of men.

A tall man straightened, and Brown recognized Thomas

Miller, the man elected wagon master by the emigrants.

"The Gordon boy just came walking in," Miller said. "He says his mule dropped of exhaustion half a mile back."

"Gordon?" the sergeant asked.

Brown stepped forward. "It's the family I told to stay at Fort Laramie. Their team was worn out, and they didn't have replacements."

Reese turned to the boy, who was slumped on the tongue of the lead wagon. "You alone, sonny?"

The boy was shivering, and a worn bridle dangled from his hand. He looked up at Reese and gulped. "Yes, sir."

"Says his folks struck out after us yesterday, but the team gave out," Miller told the sergeant. "They're at least ten miles back, to hear him tell it. They put him on the best animal two or three hours ago and told him to come for help."

Mrs. Miller hovered at her husband's elbow, clucking in disapproval. "How could Mr. Gordon endanger the boy like that?"

Miller shrugged. "Probably figured John Paul was lighter than he was and had a better chance of making it on the last mule."

The travelers had left their campfires and thronged to see what the commotion was. Miller turned to face them.

"We can't take these people with us, folks. They were told to wait at Fort Laramie, but they refused to listen."

"But we can't leave them stranded," Mrs. Carver said uncertainly.

Sergeant Reese faced the crowd. "Do you have an extra team to send back? Do you want to just give them your spare animals? Because Miller's right. Either you give them a team or room in your own wagons. That's the only way. And you all know that cuts your own chances of reaching Oregon. If any of you wants to give up a team of mules or oxen for this family, fine."

An uneasy silence fell upon the group until Miller spoke again. "Folks, I feel bad for the Gordons, but the corporal told them what was what before we left the fort. They chose to ignore his advice."

Brown glimpsed Lydia Jackson at the edge of the crowd. Her gaze never left the Gordon boy's face.

She's feeling guilty because she left them, he thought. So his first favorable impression was not amiss. The haughty Miss Jackson had a heart. The boy had come to these people for solace, and he was hearing them denounce his parents as foolish and negligent. Brown could see that it disturbed Lydia.

Mr. Paine stepped toward Miller. "Still, you can't just leave them there exposed like that."

Sergeant Reese agreed. "I'll send some men with a team of army mules to take the Gordons back to Fort Laramie. It's the best we can do."

There was a murmur of assent, and the crowd began to disperse. Brown watched Lydia, and as the men turned away, she rushed toward the boy.

"John Paul! Are you all right?"

"Miss Lydia." For the first time, John Paul Gordon looked hopeful.

"Corporal Brown," Reese called, and Mike turned away. Of course he was the logical choice for the sergeant to send on this mission. He was glad he hadn't set up his tent yet. He'd be spending the night in the saddle for sure.

❧

"Come over to the Paines' wagon. We'll feed you." Lydia led the boy along.

"Pa's gonna be madder'n spit if they send him back to the fort." John Paul hung his head as he walked with her to Dorcas's cooking fire.

"Well, we can't help that." Lydia saw that two tears had run down his cheeks, leaving paths that glittered in the firelight. "It's going to be all right." She touched his shoulder lightly, but he sniffed and pulled away.

Dorcas handed Jenny over to Lydia. "Hold the baby, dear,

and I'll take care of him. Sonny, you sit down on that box and have a bite." She scurried to fill a plate for him.

Mr. Paine poked the fire restlessly with a stick.

"This boy is asleep on his feet," Dorcas said with a frown. "Do you think Sergeant Reese really intends to take him back tonight?"

Mr. Paine shrugged. "I can ask him." He laid his stick down and ambled off across the camp.

John Paul was wolfing leftover biscuits and lukewarm stew when Paine returned with Corporal Brown beside him.

"Come on, son," Brown said. "We're heading back to your folks."

John Paul stood up, cramming half a biscuit into his mouth.

"This boy's all wrung out," Dorcas said. "Can't you let him sleep tonight and take him in the morning?"

"Well, ma'am," Brown said, "that might be good for the boy but not so good for his folks. The sergeant says we head out immediately, and I think that's wise."

"The corporal is in charge of the expedition," Mr. Paine said to Dorcas.

"That's right." Brown clapped John Paul on the shoulder. "You ready, son?"

"Let me go with him," Lydia said.

Brown turned to stare at her. "Beg pardon, miss?"

"Let me go."

"I can't do that."

"But John Paul knows me. He won't be so frightened if I'm along."

"Ma'am, we're escorting the Gordons back to Fort Laramie. Did you want to go back and stay at the fort with them?"

"Well, no, I simply thought—"

"If you come with my detail, you'll have to ride all night with four men you don't know. Aren't you the gal who didn't want to walk to the river with me?"

She felt her anger rising. The man infuriated her every time she crossed his path lately, try as she would to suppress it.

"I was thinking of the boy, Corporal."

Brown looked at John Paul critically. "He doesn't look scared to me. You think he needs a nursemaid?"

"That's uncalled for. He may not be frightened now, but—" She lowered her voice and stepped nearer. "His father's a hard man, sir."

Brown stood silent for a moment, then said, "Assuming his folks are all right when we find them, we'll see them back to Fort Laramie. That should give his father time to cool off."

"And supposing Mr. Gordon refuses to go back?"

Brown set his jaw in that implacable manner that irked her to no end. "I'll make him understand he has no choice this time."

Corporal Brown was giving notice that he could be every bit as obstinate as Mr. Gordon, and Lydia envisioned a heated melee on the plains. Her presence might shame the men into keeping their tempers, at least. "I think I should go."

"You're staying right here." He smiled, but she sensed granite behind the words.

"You can't order me around."

"Can't I?"

"No."

"You got a horse?"

Lydia swallowed. "No. I assumed—"

He laughed. "I'm sure you did. You figured I'd let you borrow a horse. Well, we don't have any sidesaddles, ma'am. We're going to ride hard, do what we have to, and come back."

He gestured for the boy to follow him and walked away, and John Paul trailed after him, his chin low on his chest. Lydia looked to Mr. Paine for support.

"Sir, you have a horse. I'm a good rider."

Mr. Paine wouldn't meet her eyes. "Best listen to the corporal."

Brown and John Paul were heading across the center of the compound, weaving between the loose cattle. Lydia took a half dozen quick strides. "Corporal Brown!"

He turned and looked at her. "This isn't a pleasure ride, Miss Jackson."

She realized several of the other travelers were watching them with avid interest. She felt her flush deepen as her ire increased. "I beg your pardon, sir. You have no call to be rude." She held his gaze, daring him to look away.

Brown took a deep breath. "I didn't intend to insult you. It's just that I have a job to do."

"And I'm keeping you from it."

He shrugged. "I'm taking three other men and six of our extra mules back to Laramie. This train's defenses will be depleted by that much until we catch up with you again. It's my responsibility to carry out my duty as quickly as possible. I'm sorry if that upsets you, but I will not change my mind."

Lydia tried to pull out a withering response, but none came to mind. In exasperation, she whirled back toward the Paines' wagon. Dorcas was feeding the cook fire, with little Jenny hanging on to her skirt.

"There you are, Lydia. Can you take Jenny for a few minutes? I don't know where Nathan's got to."

"I'm sorry. I'll look for him." Lydia scooped up the baby and walked slowly around the perimeter of the camp, crooning to Jenny and watching for Nathan.

I must remember my duty, she thought as she walked. *My loyalties are to the Paines now, not the Gordons, and I need to help Mrs. Paine.* But she couldn't forget the severe whipping Mr. Gordon had given John Paul when he'd lost his father's hatchet. Somehow she was sure the father would find a way to blame the boy if he was forced to go back to the fort. He couldn't take his frustration out on Corporal Brown. Instead he would take it out on his family.

But Brown was right. Even if she went back and stayed with the family, she couldn't stave off Mr. Gordon's rage. And she didn't want to go back. She was suddenly overcome with thankfulness for Dorcas Paine and her taciturn husband. Already she was beginning to feel at home with them, although she had yet to learn Mr. Paine's first name. It was obvious that he adored Dorcas. Lydia knew he would always put his family first, and he treated her as he would a respected member of the family. Even in refusing her the loan of his saddle horse, he was acting in her best interest.

Thank You, Lord, she breathed. *As usual, I've been headstrong.* Shame washed over her. *Forgive me for being so impulsive and so rude to Corporal Brown.* As she walked along carrying Jenny, she felt a new serenity.

She caressed Jenny's back tenderly, and the little girl snuggled against her shoulder. She found Nathan near the troopers' tents, where Brown was snapping orders for men to harness the mules that would pull the Gordons' wagon and to saddle enough mounts for John Paul and the four men who were going.

"Nathan, your mother's looking for you."

He looked up at her with huge, wistful eyes. "Wish I could go. John Paul's lucky."

She shook her head, unable to explain to him how John Paul had suffered to catch up with them and how he would no doubt suffer under his father's restless fury while waiting for another train at the fort. That was, if his family was still safe. The thought of Mrs. Gordon and the younger children huddled in the wagon while wolves howled or Indians sneaked around made her shiver.

"Go on. Eat your supper."

The boy trotted off, and she lingered a moment longer. Brown was sliding his saddle onto a fidgety chestnut gelding's back. The horse snorted and stepped away.

"There, now," Brown said softly. "Time for you and me to take a little ride, mister."

She wished she had Brown's freedom and could walk over to the army picket lines and choose whichever horse caught her fancy. The chestnut had long legs and a deep chest, and he looked like he could run for miles without being winded. How long since she'd ridden a horse like that?

She should have told Brown that she could ride as well as any man in his unit, that she wouldn't slow them down or get in the way. Not that he would have listened.

She caught herself up with surprise. Her urge to ride back to the Gordons' wagon was gone, wasn't it? How much of her desire to go with the troopers had been a longing to ride horseback again? To be free and active as she had been in childhood, to escape for a few hours the dreary existence to which she had committed herself?

She would stay with the Paines and seek every opportunity to help them. She would not fret and chafe at the agreement she had with them. And she would find time to read the small Bible she had brought along. She hadn't always made the effort to read the scripture after an exhausting day on the trail, and she regretted that. She glanced up at the star-filled sky. *Lord, help me to be a good traveler, and help me make this trip easier for the Paines, not harder.*

She realized suddenly that Brown was staring at her, and she caught her breath. He walked toward her, leading the chestnut.

"Miss Jackson, I told you I can't take you along. The subject is closed."

She lowered her gaze in embarrassment. "I'm sorry, Corporal. I can see that you're right on this matter. I was extremely rude. I hope you'll forgive me for that and for delaying you."

His tense body relaxed, and she knew he had expected another sparring round with her. "We all have strong feelings about some things. Wanting to help someone isn't a bad thing."

"Yes, well, at times I can't see the best way to do that."

"So you're content to stay here tonight?"

"Yes. God speed you on your errand."

His smile was brighter than the glowing stars above.

four

Lydia rode on the wagon seat with Dorcas the next afternoon, carefully feeding lead pellets into the hem of her extra dress, then stitching all around the hem to secure them. She had walked all morning, picking up fuel for their evening fire and watching Nathan chase butterflies with the Paines' long-eared, reddish dog, Harpy. All day she had tried not to think about Corporal Brown, but he kept coming to mind whenever she let her guard down. She liked him. She couldn't help it.

The wagon lurched as they hit a deeply rutted section of trail.

"Ouch!" Lydia sucked at her finger where the needle had stabbed it.

"Up!" Mr. Paine called, prodding the near lead ox.

"Are you all right?" Dorcas was all concern.

Lydia grimaced. "I guess I'll live." She marveled at Mr. Paine's consistency. He plodded beside his oxen all day, matching his stride to theirs and keeping the team going steadily but speaking only when necessary. Maybe that was the best kind of husband. Dependable but not very exciting. Certainly better than the choleric Mr. Sawyer, who whipped his mules on the slightest pretext. Maybe there was a medium. She wondered what a man with Mr. Paine's equanimity would be like if he had an adventurous streak.

Then again, would she ever be married? Perhaps after a teaching career, she would have that adventure. If she did have a husband, she hoped he would not be cruel and unfeeling. She couldn't bear the thought of marrying a man who was mean and autocratic. She could live with a quiet man so long as he wasn't stupid, or with a scholar if he wasn't too dull. She hoped the man she married would have a dash of chivalry. Was that too much to ask?

The thought of Corporal Brown flashed once more through her consciousness. *I mustn't allow myself to be too attracted to him,* she warned her uncooperative heart. *I have commitments, and so does he. He's a personable man with pleasing looks, spirited horses, and an air of authority. What of it? I am not here to find a husband.* Of course, a man like that would be an ironclad insurance against a dull marriage.

She knew all the young women had looked over the men of the escort, picking out the ones they believed were most eligible. Margaret Sawyer and Ellen Hadley had talked of nothing else as they walked along the dusty trail together that morning. Michael Brown and John Gleason, who was rumored to play the fiddle, seemed to be high on the list. So were young Matt Barkley and Trooper Everett Wilson. Sergeant Reese, they'd learned to their bitter disappointment, was married. His wife was awaiting his return at Fort Laramie.

"Well, I think your idea is very sound," Dorcas said, and Lydia catapulted back to the present, realizing she had stitched nearly halfway around the hem of her dress. "When you've finished, you can hold the baby, and I'll get some of Mr. Paine's lead and stitch my claret skirt."

"Hello, ladies." Both women looked up at the greeting. Brown was riding up alongside them from behind. The fractious bay mare tossed her head with a snort, sending her coal black mane rippling. Brown put his gloved hand to the brim of his hat, smiling broadly.

"You're back already!" Dorcas's eyes were wide in disbelief.

"Yes, ma'am. The Gordons were closer to the fort than they were to us. It was almost midnight when we found them. They hadn't seen anyone since Fort Laramie except the mail rider who passed us yesterday. We hitched our mules up to their wagon right away and took them in."

"Driving all night in the dark?" Dorcas shook her head.

"Yes, ma'am. We rode into the fort at first light, got a hot breakfast, and turned around to come back."

Lydia's heart pounded, and she told herself it was due to the closeness of his beautiful mare. She wished that just once she could ride the bay. Brown must have switched mounts when he caught up with the herd of livestock that followed the train. Her gaze drifted from the horse's sleek head and delicately pricked ears and rested on Brown's face.

"The Gordons must be thankful you came," she said, eager for news and determined not to start another argument with him.

Brown winced. "Well, Mr. Gordon's not too happy with me, sad to say. I had my men put his last mule down. It was in terrible distress."

"You must be tired," Dorcas said.

Lydia glanced at him furtively. Whiskers darkened his firm jaw, giving him a dangerous air, and there were deep shadows beneath his eyes.

Brown shrugged. "Part of the job, ma'am." He nodded with approval toward Lydia's sewing project. "Glad to see you've taken my suggestion."

Dorcas's eyes widened. "*Your* suggestion? Why, Lydia, you didn't tell me this clever gentleman invented the idea."

Brown laughed. "Hardly my invention, ma'am. Ladies out here have been doing it for some time."

Lydia lowered her head and concentrated on her stitching.

"You're an asset to the company, Corporal Brown." Dorcas smiled up at him sweetly.

"Thank you, ma'am. Oh, by the way, Miss Jackson—" He held out a two-pound sack, and Lydia reached for it in wonder. "Mrs. Gordon was extremely glad to see John Paul come back safe, and she asked me to give you this. She said you would understand."

Lydia held the bag to her nose and breathed in the rich aroma. "Coffee." She handed it to Dorcas. "Would you put that with the family supplies, please?"

"With pleasure. Mr. Paine will be delighted."

Brown leaned toward them from the saddle as the mare kept pace. "The boy was fine when I left them. I told his pa he ought to be proud of him."

Lydia nodded. Looking into his deep, brown eyes made her pulse accelerate and her cheeks flush. She looked straight ahead. "Thank you."

"Well, it was about all we could do." He grinned. "Don't put too much lead in there, now. The troopers will be disappointed." He tipped his hat and spurred his horse forward until he was hidden from their view by the next wagon.

Dorcas was smiling, her face pink with pleasure. "That is a very nice young man, Lydia."

"I'm not so sure."

"Why, my dear, you don't think he's nice?"

"He has an impudent side."

"Oh, he's friendly, and he likes a joke, but he seems sincere."

"Can two people make each other angry and still like each other?" Lydia asked, and Dorcas looked at her with injured surprise.

"Corporal Brown was perfectly civil just now."

"I suppose he was, but we've had a few moments when he made my blood boil. Perhaps I was unjust."

Lydia frowned, jabbing her needle through the fabric. It was true he was handsome and clever, and he seemed to have a compassionate vein, as well. Was she taking offense too easily? When she considered his motives each time they had crossed swords verbally, she had to admit he hadn't been insufferable. He had a heightened sense of duty, and that had caused their biggest flare-up. She feared it would be easy to let herself be drawn to the corporal, and she mustn't do that. She needed to keep her emotions in check. After all, she had a job ahead of her. Perhaps that was why her mind told her she had taken a dislike to him.

"Mr. Paine and the sergeant were having a cup of coffee last evening, and Mr. Paine asked about Corporal Brown's horses," Dorcas said.

"His horses?" Against her will, Lydia gave her attention to Dorcas.

"Surely you've noticed that Brown's horses are better than all the others. Why, most of the troopers are riding mules, which is all well and good. They're hardy and they're easy keepers, but—" Lydia waved one hand, and Dorcas trailed to a stop. "Don't you care about the horses? I thought you loved them. You said your father bred fine carriage horses."

"Corporal Brown is in charge of their remounts." Lydia hoped to steer her smoothly back to the topic.

"That's right. When a man needs a new horse, he has to go to Corporal Brown for it."

"And that's why he has the best horse. That seems a bit self-serving, doesn't it?"

"Well, the sergeant told Mr. Paine that Brown keeps the horses in good shape for the officers. He rides the most obstreperous animals in the herd."

"Also the most beautiful," Lydia said thoughtfully.

"Can he help it if that gorgeous bay is more ornery than the stubbornest mule? He's training it to be a good, steady mount. Sergeant Reese said that when they get new animals, it's Brown's job to try them out and assign them to the men according to their ability and the animals' temperaments."

Lydia smiled. "Exactly as you say, Dorcas. *He* rides the ornery ones." Even as she reached for the baby, she knew it was a cutting and undeserved assessment of the corporal. "Here, let me hold Jenny. Your arms must be tired."

As the wagon creaked along, Lydia hummed softly to lull Jenny to sleep. Dorcas fetched her workbag, but she decided she couldn't sew after all, with the wagon lurching so, and took out her crocheting instead. As she worked, she prattled on about the disappointing array of supplies at Fort Laramie and the scandalously meager wardrobe of Mrs. Carver and her daughters in the wagon ahead of them.

Lydia found her thoughts straying again to the handsome corporal. It was the mare that drew her attention, she told herself. The rider held less than no interest for her. She would rather drink water from the Platte River than engage Corporal Brown in conversation.

But that wasn't true—far from it.

Lord, help me! she prayed in silent exasperation. *I'm a grown woman, on my way to fill a demanding position, and here I am getting starry-eyed over a dashing man. Help me to focus on what's ahead and to put aside thoughts of Michael Brown. I don't see that he fits into Your plan for me.*

❧

The first ford over the Platte was a time of testing. The travelers had crossed the river many times in Nebraska Territory, but it was more treacherous here. Since leaving Fort Laramie they had resorted to ferries when a crossing was necessary. But now they were beyond the ferries, and the emigrants were on their own.

The troopers had been through the harrowing experience before and showed the families how to waterproof their loads. Early in the morning, Brown and Barkley tested the ford. Halfway across, the water rose to their mounts' bellies, but Brown was confident the oxen could make the ford without losing their footing. Oxen couldn't swim and pull wagons the way horses could. If the water was too deep, they would have to unload all the wagons and float the goods across in a few watertight wagon boxes, dismantle the other ox-drawn wagons, float the parts across, swim the animals over, and reassemble the train.

But it was mid-July, and the river was fairly low. Most of the men in the company seemed competent with their teams, and there should be no serious problems. Brown sent Barkley back to report to Sergeant Reese that the crossing was not too risky. The settlers would need to keep their teams moving; that was the main thing.

Mike rode on to scout the trail ahead for two or three miles. He spotted a small band of Sioux camped beside the river, but he had no fear of them. The wagon train had four times as many men and ought to pass the Indian camp without incident, unless the Sioux swarmed out to beg the travelers to trade. The wagon train would be well advised to chain their stock up tonight and post a heavy guard, however.

He rode to the top of the next knoll and stopped, looking out over the endless prairie. Bushy yellow and purple flowers grew all across the plain. From a distance, the colored patches were resplendent, waving in the wind. They didn't have masses of flowers like this where he grew up in Tennessee. Martha would have loved to see them.

He took a deep, careful breath. It didn't hurt so much to think about her now. Out here, under the limitless sky, he was able to talk to God about it and to forgive himself for leaving her and Billy behind.

The mare tossed her head and pawed the ground. Mike turned her around and loosened the reins just a hair, and she took off at a canter, toward the ford.

five

Lydia avoided Brown for the next week, but that wasn't difficult. He seemed to draw a lot of scouting details, riding forward of the train for long periods. Occasionally she saw him across the compound early in the morning, drinking coffee with the other troopers, but then he rode out and was gone all day.

One evening he dropped by to speak to Mr. Paine but declined Dorcas's offer of supper. More often, Mr. Paine would go join the men at the escort's fire in the evening.

The days settled into the routine of the trail. Lydia found her life with the Paines pleasant compared to her stay with the Gordons, but monotony was inevitable. She walked sometimes with the other women or gathered fuel with Nathan. She carried Jenny for short periods or sat on the wagon box holding her to give Dorcas a respite. She was becoming fond of the two children.

When the train halted for nooning and when they circled for the night, each family member began his chores. Mr. Paine lit the fire and tended the oxen and his horse, Beauty. Lydia took care of Jenny and brought water, while Nathan gathered fuel. Dorcas immediately began preparing the meal. Most days Trooper Gleason found one excuse or another to stop by their camp spot, and Lydia was afraid he harbored hopes that he might win her heart.

In the long, mindless hours of trudging along the trail, Lydia thought about what lay ahead. Oregon seemed farther away than ever. Sometimes it seemed they would never get out of this vast, dusty plain. Other times she summoned a bright vision of herself teaching eager children. It would be a worthwhile, satisfying life.

She walked along one torrid afternoon with three of the

young women close to her age. Frances Bailey's family had joined the train at Fort Laramie, and Lydia felt an affinity for her. The Baileys seemed a bit more refined than some of the others in the company and had been faithful in attending chapel services at Fort Laramie. This morning Lydia had gone early to the Baileys' wagon to invite Frances to fetch water with her and had found the girl reading from a battered volume of William Blake's poetry. At that moment, Lydia knew she and Frances had much in common, and she was eager to learn more about her new friend.

Margaret Sawyer was the oldest girl in her large family, and she escaped the range of her mother's voice whenever possible. Margaret was often required to look after a brood of younger siblings but occasionally was able to slip off and socialize with other young people, especially Ellen Hadley.

Ellen was promised to marry Margaret's eldest brother, Charlie Sawyer. She was seventeen, and according to Margaret, Ellen's parents weren't crazy about seeing their daughter married so young. In Lydia's opinion, it was the intended groom who raised the Hadleys' objections. Charlie was an immature nineteen, given to practical jokes and horseplay. Lydia had trouble seeing him as husband material. The Sawyers and the Hadleys had been neighbors in Ohio and traveled west together. Ellen said her parents had agreed to allow the wedding once they reached Oregon.

"I'll be eighteen, anyway," she'd said airily.

Jenny was napping in the wagon when Frances, Margaret, and Ellen came to coax Lydia to walk with them.

"Jenny will sleep for a couple of hours, and Nathan will stay with his father," Dorcas told her. "Go and enjoy yourself."

Lydia wasn't sure she wanted to get too close to Margaret and Ellen. She had experienced their idle chatter before, with the result that she now knew more about the inner workings of their families than she wanted to know. But Frances's look held such a wistful appeal that she decided to go.

"Just let me get my chip basket."

Margaret laughed. "I've got mine. Ma says I can't go off and leave her with the little ones without bringing home fuel for the cook fire."

They walked along slowly so as not to outdistance the wagons, stooping frequently for dried buffalo chips.

Ellen ran a finger around the collar of her cotton dress. "If it weren't for this breeze, we'd all bake to a crisp."

"We should have brought a water skin," Margaret agreed. "I feel like I'm going to shrivel up and mummify."

Lydia glanced at Frances and returned the shy smile Frances gave her. She was about to ask her how she liked Blake's poetry when Margaret said, "Don't look. Troopers coming up behind us."

Ellen giggled.

"I just pretend I don't notice them," Frances said softly.

"Ladies!"

It was amiable Trooper John Gleason and another man whose acquaintance Lydia had so far avoided. He and Gleason reined their mules to a pace that matched that of the young women.

"Miss Sawyer, Miss Hadley," said Gleason. "And Miss Jackson."

"Good day, Private Gleason," Lydia said. She was not surprised that Gleason had made it his business to know the names of all the single young women.

"Haven't met this young lady," said Gleason.

Frances stared at the ground, blushing.

"Oh, that's Frances Bailey," Margaret said with a saucy smile. "She's quiet as a church mouse."

"Yes," said Ellen. "She generally hides in her pa's wagon, but we dragged her out for a constitutional."

Gleason laughed. "Have you ladies all met Trooper Stedman?"

"Why, no," Ellen said. She and Margaret called a merry greeting to the second man.

"Ladies." The trooper tipped his hat and smiled at them boldly.

"Trooper Gleason, is it true you have a fiddle?" Margaret asked.

"Yes, miss. One of these nights we'll have us some dancin'."

"Oh, how about tonight?" Margaret squealed, and Lydia wished the dusty soil would part and swallow her whole.

Gleason shrugged. "Folks'll be tired tonight. Sometime when we're going to stop a bit, maybe."

"I hope it's soon," Ellen said, her eyes shining.

"You just want to dance with Charlie," Margaret said.

"I'd dance with most anybody about now," Ellen retorted. "I hardly ever see Charlie. He's always off minding the stock."

"What, you gals not getting enough exercise during the day?" Stedman asked, and Margaret and Ellen giggled.

Frances was lagging behind, and Lydia slowed her steps, as well. She didn't want the men to consider her a part of the flirtation, harmless though it may be.

Gleason's voice carried easily. "Well, Pete, when we get an evening for dancin', you'll have to make sure these ladies don't lack for partners."

"It will be a pleasure," Stedman said. "Why, I expect so many gents will stand in line that you ladies will dance until dawn."

The men touched their hats and urged their mules into a trot. Sergeant Reese was coming down the line of wagons toward them, and Lydia guessed the two troopers didn't want him to see them loitering.

"He is just too handsome," Margaret said dreamily.

"Which one?" Ellen asked.

"Either."

Frances winced at Lydia, and Lydia smiled. "Long weeks on the trail can enhance a man's looks," she whispered, and Frances convulsed in silent laughter.

"I wouldn't mind dancing with Trooper Stedman," Ellen said.

"Too bad Gleason can't fiddle and dance at the same time," Margaret added, and Lydia couldn't hold back her laugh.

"Well, there!" Ellen cried. "You can take a joke, after all. You're usually as sober as a judge who lost his gavel."

Lydia smiled ruefully, wondering if perhaps she was too somber. Sergeant Reese had passed the other two troopers and was cantering his gray horse toward them. He passed a few yards from the girls, and Lydia turned to watch the gelding's springy gait.

"The sergeant's married," Margaret said with evident disappointment.

Lydia jerked her head around to face westward again. "I wasn't ogling the sergeant. I was looking at his horse."

"His horse!" Ellen giggled. "That's likely!"

"I'd love to have a chance to ride some of the horses these cavalrymen have," Lydia said.

"Can you ride?" Frances asked. "I've never learned."

"Oh, yes," Lydia said. "I used to ride a lot, when my father was alive."

"I'd be afraid," Frances declared. The other girls laughed.

"It's not so hard," said Margaret. "I used to ride our plow horse out to the pasture and back. Now all we've got are those nasty oxen."

"What sort of horse did your father have?" Frances asked, looking at Lydia with huge, admiring eyes.

"He had lots of horses." Lydia saw glances pass between the other girls, and she wished she hadn't said it. She could see that they were wondering whether to believe her or not. "My father raised horses. He trained them for saddle and for carriage teams. His clients came from all over Connecticut, and some even came up from New York to buy at our farm."

"Sounds as if you had it pretty soft," Margaret said.

Ellen clucked her tongue and frowned at Margaret.

Lydia shrugged. "That was a long time ago."

"What happened?" Frances asked.

Lydia hesitated, but Frances at least seemed sympathetic. "Father died. We had a fire, and he was trying to get the horses out of the barn. They were his fortune, you see. The stallion especially. Father was determined to save him." She felt the tears pricking at her eyelids, though it had been more than five years. "He told me to wait while he went in for Jubel."

They walked in silence for several paces, then Margaret prodded, "And?"

"The roof of the barn collapsed. He didn't get out."

Frances's hot fingers clasped Lydia's for a moment. "I'm sorry," she whispered.

"Did the horse survive?" Margaret asked.

"Margaret! That's insensitive of you!" Ellen cried.

Lydia swallowed hard. "No. No, Jubel didn't make it, either."

"What about your mother?" Frances's eyes were also glistening with tears, and Lydia managed a weak smile, wondering how she had allowed herself to be persuaded to tell this tale.

"My mother died when I was quite young. So after the fire I was an orphan."

The other three girls sighed, and Frances slipped her arm around Lydia. "You poor thing. Is that why you came west?"

Lydia smiled. "No. I went to live with my aunt after that. I was fifteen years old, and she thought I ought to finish my education."

"Really?" Ellen's eyebrows arched in surprise. "Mine was finished long before I reached fifteen."

"Well, it was a bit different there, I expect," Lydia said. Although she now shared these young women's state of abject poverty, it hadn't always been so. Her memories of the comfortable old home at the horse farm and of her aunt's mansion in Hartford were painful now.

"Anyway," she said briskly, "my aunt picked out the school she thought was most suitable and sent me there. I attended for three years, but I didn't have many chances to ride anymore."

"No horsemanship classes?" Ellen asked with a chuckle.

"Wouldn't that be grand?" Margaret's giggle rose once more to an annoying tone. "Do they teach fine ladies to ride in Connecticut?"

"I expect they do," Lydia said, "but not at my school. In the city park, we used to see ladies out riding. They had fine velvet habits and sidesaddles, of course."

"Of course," Ellen said, her eyes twinkling. "And no doubt were escorted by gentlemen in caped coats and top hats."

"Certainly."

"Wouldn't that be lovely to see?" Frances sighed.

"Too bad your school wasn't fine enough to teach you that," said Margaret.

Lydia knew how dearly Miss Clarkson would have liked to add equestrian classes to her curriculum, but alas, the school would have needed a wealthy benefactor for that. As it was, they'd had other innovative courses.

"My teacher was quite progressive," she said. "She was a great proponent of decorative arts and physical education."

"What's that?" asked Margaret.

Frances's eyes were wide. "Is that where you learn all the insides of the body?"

"No," Lydia laughed. "It's where you exercise for your health and learn agility and coordination."

Margaret blinked at her as if she couldn't imagine what Lydia meant.

"Sounds high-falutin'," Ellen said. "We got the three Rs through sixth grade, and that was it."

"I learned to embroider and play the organ," Frances said. Her timid glance told Lydia she considered making this information public a risk.

Lydia smiled at her. "I'd love to hear you play sometime."

"We had to leave the instrument behind."

"Ah. Well, perhaps there will be one in Oregon."

"Perhaps," Frances agreed. "They say some folks send fine furniture around Cape Horn to Oregon by ship."

Lydia squeezed Frances's hand and let it go. "I've enjoyed the company, ladies, but I must see if Mrs. Paine needs me. Jenny has probably finished her nap by now."

As she hastened her steps toward the Paines' wagon, she heard Margaret say, "Ain't we grand?"

Frances's troubled reply came soft but firm. "I think she's wonderful."

"Do you believe that about the fire and all?" Margaret asked.

Lydia hurried on, biting her lip. It would have been much better to have kept her thoughts to herself. Now those who believed her would pity her, and those who didn't would think she'd invented a story to draw sympathy.

six

Mike knew they were close to Independence Rock, the half-way point for most of the emigrants. They would leave the muddy Platte and follow the Sweetwater upstream toward the mountains. It was a point of change, and the settlers were filled with excitement. But first they had to negotiate the Platte one last time.

The troopers rode alongside the teams, shouting encouragement to the drivers. It was their third river crossing in five days, and each ford had its treacheries. Now the Platte was swollen from rain in the mountains.

One moment the Anderson family's team strode confidently in two inches of murky water; the next they were breast-deep and floundering, with the wagon careening crazily behind them.

Mike sat on his mount—a big, powerful mule—watching in exasperation.

"Get them over!" he yelled to Trooper Wilson, who was trying to grab the bridle of one of the wheelers. "Three feet to your right, and you'll be fine!"

To Mike's relief, the off mules gained solid footing. The team soon lumbered up the far bank with the wagon intact.

Mike sighed. He had spent most of the day in and out of the water, soaked to his knees. The mule he called Buster was steadier than most of the horses and reliable for this work.

The pioneers were grim-faced, and many had lightened their wagons. Some of the furniture they were trying to tote to Oregon amazed him.

"You'll never get that article over the Rockies, ma'am, let alone the Cascades," he told Mrs. Hunter, as two of his men helped her husband unload an oak credenza. "Trust me. Save your energy for the things you need."

"We should have sold it in New Jersey," her husband said bitterly. "Travel light. That's what they told us."

Mike left them and headed for where the Paines waited. Their wagon was one that had been taken apart and water-proofed with hides and grease and used in the ferrying. Josiah Paine had gone back and forth all day with the troopers, helping others, and Mike felt he deserved extra help now to ensure that his goods and his family passed safely over the Platte.

He and Paine began to load crates, bedding, and pans into the wagon box. Nathan, Lydia, and Dorcas brought them bundles to stow.

A flash of color caught Mike's eye, and he looked up to see Gleason riding his mule up from the ford, carrying an armful of pink and lavender flowers.

"Well, John," he said and laughed. "What are you up to?"

Gleason smiled. "Thought I'd cheer up the ladies. Mrs. Paine, Miss Jackson, this is but a preview of the lovely country across the river."

Lydia laughed, reaching out to take the flowers from him. "Lovely country exactly like the country we left when we crossed six miles downstream, I take it."

Dorcas frowned. "Now, Lydia, be gracious. This gentleman took time to pick us a nosegay, and isn't it fine? Thank you, Trooper Gleason."

Mike chuckled. "Miss Jackson would have liked it better if you'd brought her some of those burdocks we saw growing over the hill yonder for the stew pot."

"Burdocks?" Lydia asked eagerly.

Her face told him she was ravenous. The few root vegetables they'd brought had probably been eaten weeks ago, and there had been nothing fresh available at Fort Laramie.

"Take it easy, Miss Jackson," Gleason said with a smile. "Don't get all het up about burdocks. They're several miles ahead, and by the time we get you folks over the river, it'll be most dark. No root digging tonight."

Dorcas had perked up, too. "I'd love to get hold of some of those roots. It would make a nice change."

The Paines and the Hunters were the only two families left to cross. This ford was taking longer than most, and unpacking and transferring the loads was disheartening. Miller and Reese had agreed to camp just over the river for the night to allow the people to put their things back in order.

"Time for you ladies to cross," Mike said.

"I'll take Nathan with me," said Mr. Paine. "Mrs. Paine can ride Beauty over and carry Jenny."

"I'll take the little one for you," Mike offered. He caught a shocked glance from Lydia as he reached for the baby. She probably thought he'd never held a baby before and would drop Jenny into the swirling water. Jenny looked up at him as Dorcas lifted her and reached a chubby hand toward his face. Mike smiled. The little girl's clothing was clean and her hair combed. He pulled her to his chest as he would a precious treasure. "Say, John, Miss Jackson needs a ride over."

"Well, I—" Lydia looked around quickly, as if searching for an alternative. The only other trooper still on this side of the Platte was Barkley, and he was speaking with Mr. Paine about guiding the oxen across.

"Why, miss, I'd be honored," Gleason said, flushing beneath his tan.

Lydia hesitated, then nodded. "Thank you, I appreciate that."

Gleason slipped his boot from his near stirrup, and she raised her foot to the iron, then reached up and grasped Gleason's wrist, swinging herself up in a graceful arc and landing gently behind the saddle.

She's done that before. A stab of envy quickly replaced Mike's surprise as he saw her hands creep reluctantly onto Gleason's shoulders. Just for a moment he wished he had offered to take Lydia himself and left Jenny to her mother.

Against his better sense, he urged Buster close to Gleason's mule for a moment and whispered, "Don't y'all be afraid to hang on, now. We'd hate to have to pull you out of the Platte."

Lydia scowled at him, and he winked, then headed Buster for the water, holding little Jenny cuddled tight against his shoulder. Buster stepped awkwardly into the murky water, and Mike let the mule find his balance. Dorcas's horse stepped in without balking. Mike looked back. As Gleason's mule plunged in, Lydia suddenly grabbed the trooper around the waist and clung to him. Gleason's grin told Mike that John's strategy had worked, and he'd managed to scare Lydia into embracing him. Yes, John was happy to have the plum assignment.

That's all right, Mike told himself. *It's not every day a man gets to hold a sweet-smelling baby.*

ra

Mrs. Paine offered supper to the three troopers who had helped them get their wagon and family across the river. Lydia accepted the men's eager response with resignation.

Most of the other women had been on the north bank for hours, and Mrs. Carver invited Dorcas to cook at her fire. It had burned down to a fine bed of coals, and Dorcas gratefully rummaged for her pans in the wagon box and began to fix supper. Lydia helped, wishing they had some of those elusive burdocks. Somehow she would get some tomorrow, no matter what.

Barkley, Gleason, and Brown sat on crates, talking lazily with Mr. Paine.

"We'll feed them first," Dorcas told Lydia in a low voice. "I don't have enough plates for us all to eat at once." She gave Jenny a dry biscuit to gnaw on while they hurriedly prepared the meal.

Frances appeared in the twilight with a pan of fresh-baked cornbread. "Mama sent this over. She made extra for you and the Hunters."

"Bless you, child!" Dorcas cried. "Give your mother a kiss for me, and tell her I'll return the pan in the morning."

Frances smiled. "Is there anything I can do? You seem to have some extra mouths to feed this evening."

"My dear, if you could find an extra coffee mug for us to

borrow, it would put us in good order."

Frances hastened to fetch a mug and then offered to watch Jenny. Lydia and Mrs. Paine soon had the meal ready. Lydia filled tin plates with stew for the men and Nathan and carried them to the circle before the Paines' wagon while Dorcas poured coffee.

"Thank you," Gleason said, grinning up at Lydia. He obviously thought she was mad about him, after the way she had shamelessly held on to him during the river crossing. How could she tell him it was only because the horse had lunged so violently that she feared for her life?

"So you fellows have been out here quite a spell," Mr. Paine said as Lydia handed him his supper.

"Oh, I've only been with the Seventh about a year," Gleason said, "but Matt and the corporal have been here a lot longer."

"It's been about five years for me now." Brown accepted his plate with a cheerful nod. "Matt's the one who's practically a native."

Barkley grinned. "Yeah, my folks left Massachusetts when I was just a kid. I grew up in the Green River Valley, about five miles from Fort Bridger."

"Did you ever meet Jim Bridger?" Dorcas asked as she made the rounds with hot coffee.

"Several times," Barkley said. "He's quite the character."

"And how did you get your education in the wilderness?" Dorcas asked. Lydia knew she was concerned about schooling for Nathan and Jenny once they settled on their claim in Oregon.

"Well, I'd had some back East, and my mother kept us kids at it out here. We didn't have many books, but we got along. She had us scratch our sums in the dirt sometimes, because we didn't have paper to waste. Anytime my father had a chance to trade for a book, he did."

Dorcas nodded. "Your mother must have been a courageous and resourceful woman."

"Yes, ma'am, she was."

"We had a dame school when I was a lad," Mr. Paine revealed, and Lydia looked at him in surprise. He rarely said more than five words in an evening, but when he did speak, it was with flawless grammar. She hovered, wanting to hear more.

"I only went through four grades, but it's served me well. How about you, Corporal?" he asked.

"I had a little schooling back home," Brown said. "Not as much as some."

"Probably more than me," Gleason said. "There wasn't any school where my pappy settled in Arkansas. He turned and looked at Lydia. "How about yourself, Miss Jackson? Did you have any teaching?"

She hesitated. "I was tutored at home, and then—"

"And then I suppose they sent you to a finishing school," Gleason said with a laugh.

"Well. . .yes. Miss Clarkson's Seminary for Young Ladies, in Hartford, Connecticut."

"There, now," said Mr. Paine.

Brown was smiling. "For young ladies, yet."

Barkley nodded. "No hoydens allowed."

"In Hartford, Connecticut," Gleason said.

"Yes." Lydia wasn't sure she liked the way the conversation was going. The troopers seemed ready to make fun of her.

"Let me guess," Brown said. "You learned to play the dulcimer and stitch petit point."

She eyed the corporal suspiciously, expecting his sarcasm to blossom. "We did study music and embroidery. Also archery. Developing manual dexterity is important."

"Oh, of course." He smiled and sipped his coffee.

"They do that where I come from, too," Gleason said.

"Really?" Lydia asked with misgiving.

"Yeah, but instead of archery, the ladies chop wood and hoe the corn patch."

"Good for manual dexterity, I expect," Barkley said with a laugh.

Gleason laughed, too, and Mr. Paine smiled good-naturedly,

but Lydia didn't find it humorous.

"Take it easy on Miss Jackson, boys," Brown said. "She had a chance to learn something, and she took it."

"There's nothing to belittle in that," Mr. Paine agreed.

Barkley smiled ruefully. "Sorry, Miss Jackson."

Frances had been sitting all the while on a quilt with Jenny, and she asked dreamily, "Did you learn to speak French at Miss Clarkson's?"

"Latin," Lydia said.

"Oh, of course, Latin." Gleason's affable smile made her want to scream.

"That will do you so much good out here," said Barkley. "Especially if we run into some ancient Italians."

"Well, Matt, you know, them Arapaho are always roamin'." Gleason hooted at his own pun.

Lydia felt her upper lip quiver and bit it.

Brown was watching her, and he rose, passing his mug to Lydia. "If it's not too much trouble, Miss Jackson, might I have a drop more coffee?"

"Of course." She went to retrieve the coffeepot, and Brown followed her.

"Don't let the fellows bother you," he said softly. "They're just having fun. They don't get a chance very often. It's true they don't have the best parlor manners, but sitting down with a nice family like this will do them a world of good."

"You're the one who should teach them manners, Corporal Brown." A lump was forming in Lydia's throat, and she tried to swallow it down. She ought to be able to laugh along with them, but the memories of the past hurt too much. She glared at him, hoping she could escape his presence before her tears spilled over. "Your men are churlish, and there have been moments when I thought you were the same."

Brown's merry laugh exploded. "I've never met that word outside a book. Perhaps you'd better introduce us properly." He turned to Paine. "I do beg your pardon if we've spoken out of turn, sir. Miss Jackson thinks we're churlish."

"Not you, Corporal," Mr. Paine said with a frown.

"Yes, me, too."

"Oh, no, miss," said Gleason. "He's from Tennessee."

Lydia sent Gleason a glare that she hoped would give him frostbite. She gathered her skirts and turned toward the wagon, ignoring the men's riotous laughter.

seven

Trooper Gleason appeared in the center of the camp after supper with his fiddle, and Mr. Adams soon joined him with a mouth organ. The girls were giddy when the dancing began, and even the grown-ups joined in. Mr. Paine took a turn with Dorcas, while Lydia hung back in the shadows, holding Jenny. Finally Dorcas came and coaxed her to join the fun.

"Come on, dear. I'll put Jenny to bed and stay near the wagon in case she cries."

Lydia hesitated, then moved toward the center of the corral. One of the troopers immediately claimed her hand, and she danced for an hour, changing partners with each new tune. She was surprised to find that she was enjoying herself with the other young people. But Corporal Brown was nowhere to be seen.

She told herself she wasn't disappointed and resolved not to ask about him, but it didn't matter. Margaret Sawyer pulled her aside, her eyes glowing. "Too bad the corporal has sentry duty tonight. I'd give anything to dance with him! Oh well, Private Wilson is a passable dancer."

"Isn't that Trooper Stedman dancing with Ellen?" Lydia asked. "Where's Charlie?"

Margaret snorted. "Yonder with Tim Anderson. He's madder'n a hornet. Ellen's danced with Pete Stedman three times tonight!"

Lydia decided the less said the better on that topic. "Oh, look, Minnie Carver's dancing with Dr. Nichols!"

Margaret laughed. "Her sister Jean got the first hour, and Minnie's got this hour."

"Are they watching the children turnabout?" Lydia asked, puzzled.

"No, they've only got one decent dress between them, and

they had to switch off." Margaret turned a bright smile on the cavalryman approaching them.

"Miss Jackson, isn't it?" the trooper asked, looking past Margaret at Lydia.

"I. . .yes."

"I'm David Farley. Would you do me the honor?"

"Well, I—" Lydia glanced apologetically toward Margaret, but the girl had already turned away and was accepting the attentions of another trooper, so Lydia smiled and took Farley's hand.

It was not an unpleasant evening, she thought, though none of the troopers overly impressed her. Most were homesick young fellows who had been away from their families for months or even years and longed to have someone to talk to. Lydia prided herself on being a good listener. She said very little about herself but drew the men out about their families and the rough life they led in the cavalry.

When the party broke up and Gleason stopped playing, Lydia saw him looking around, and she feared he was searching for her. She slipped away and went back to the wagon. Dorcas was dozing on her pallet with Jenny curled beside her, and Nathan snored gently. Mr. Paine was tending the fire. He nodded to her and stepped over the wagon tongue with Harpy on his heels. Lydia knew they would make their nightly inspection of the family's livestock.

She pulled her blankets and carpetbag out of the wagon and made her bed with the bag as her pillow. Before she settled down, she reached deep inside it. Under her extra clothing was her Bible. She felt around a bit more until paper crackled between her fingers, and she drew out a creased and worn envelope.

It was too dark to read, but she held it close to her heart. Dancing had been fun, but she wasn't out to find a husband. It was because of this letter that she had set out on this arduous journey. She knew it almost by heart. It was the agreement that pulled her to Oregon.

The loss of her parents and later her aunt had set her adrift, alone in the world. Then came the discovery that Aunt Moriah had spent all her resources on Lydia's education. Lydia remembered the weeks of terrifying hopelessness when she had asked one family friend after another for advice on finding a position, but none could help her.

At last she had turned to her beloved former teacher. Miss Clarkson had allowed her to stay at the seminary for three months without paying board. In return, Lydia assisted with some of the lower classes and cleaned the classrooms. At last Miss Clarkson had presented an offer. A town in Oregon wanted a schoolteacher, one who could set up an academy that taught a classical curriculum. It would be an arduous trip, and the pay was low for a demanding job.

"The teacher must agree to one year's service and must not marry during the term of her contract," read the paper the school board had sent. At the time, that restriction had seemed irrelevant. Lydia had no prospects for marriage, and the security of a teaching contract seemed the best possible solution to her problems.

Dear God, Lydia prayed haltingly, as she clutched the envelope containing her copy of the contract, *You have given me this opportunity. Please help me to live up to the terms I agreed to. Help me to be a good teacher and to help many children learn. And help me not to wish for a different life.*

☙

Mike ambled slowly around the rope corral the troopers had erected to pen in their mounts for the night. Private Haines was making the circuit of the corral in the other direction. Usually the stock was confined within the circle of the wagons for safety at night, but tonight that space had been appropriated for dancing. The strains of Gleason's fiddle had faded, and it was quiet now. The mules stamped and snorted as they vied for the dry grass. Mike watched outward as he walked, searching for sounds and movements that didn't belong in the dark, peaceful scene.

As he came around the side nearest the wagons, he saw a form coming toward him.

"Who's there?" Mike called softly.

"It's me—Paine."

"Evenin'." Mike waited for him.

"Thought I might find you out here," Paine said.

"Walk with me, sir," Mike replied, and they fell into step around the circle. The horses and mules cropped the grass without taking notice of them.

"I've got a riding mare," Paine said after a moment.

"I noticed her. Good, stout horse."

"Yes, well, she picked up some nettles today. I plucked them out of her leg, and I don't think it's serious, but she worries at the spot. Don't want her to rub the skin off."

"I've got something," Mike said. "It's in one of our supply wagons. Better than lard. I'll get it for you when someone relieves me."

"I'm obliged."

They strolled on in a new sense of companionship. A horse nickered and stepped toward the rope barrier. In the faint light, Mike could make out the markings of the bay mare he liked to ride. She thrust her nose over the rope and snuffled.

"Big baby." Mike stroked her muzzle. He and Paine kept walking, and the mare lowered her head to graze. "There's still a lot of rough country between here and Oregon," Mike said. "Be hard for the missus and the young ones."

"Mrs. Paine isn't one to complain when things get difficult."

"That's true," Mike said. "She's held up better than a lot of folks. Are you figuring to farm in Oregon?"

Paine was silent for a moment before he answered. "I want a place of my own. A place where Dorcas and the young 'uns can live peaceful."

Mike sighed. "Well, if you're not too picky, you might find it. Most of the best land is taken, but there are still homesteads available."

"I'd never be able to own a farm of any size back East. But

out here, they say any hardworking man can make a go of it."

They paced on in silence, and Mike stayed alert to the night sounds.

"What about you, Corporal? What do you want out here?" Paine asked.

"Well now, that's a question. Everything I wanted is gone now."

"How's that?"

Mike took a long, deep breath. "My family. Lost them near two years ago. I was at Fort Bridger and didn't know about it for months. My wife and little boy, that is."

"I'm sorry."

"To tell you the truth, I'd like to have a home again. Don't expect to see it happen, though."

"You never know what God will do."

Mike nodded. "That's so. Thank you for reminding me."

They walked on in silence. Two troopers approached from the camp, and Mike greeted them. The two new guards started out in opposite directions around the corral. Mike and Mr. Paine walked back toward the wagons together. Mike struck a match and lit a lantern at the back of one of the wagons. He rummaged in his chest of remedies for the livestock and came out with a tin of salve.

"Put some of that on your mare's leg. I don't know if it helps the healing, but it tastes bad enough to keep her from licking it."

Paine nodded. "I thank you."

Mike smiled then. "There's one other thing I'd really like to see out here."

"What's that?"

"That gal traveling with you—"

"Miss Jackson?"

"That's the one," Mike said. "She takes herself far too seriously. I'd like to see her laugh."

❧

The next morning Mike rode ahead of the train to evaluate

the conditions between their overnight stop and Independence Rock. They could be there by midafternoon, he judged, if nothing unforeseen delayed them.

He reined the bay mare to a halt beneath the huge rock, staring westward toward Devil's Gate. It was here that he and three others had made a stand against a trio of renegades two years back, and one of his fellow troopers had been killed. That was a black moment, and he'd wondered if he would survive his tour of duty in Wyoming Territory. He was a happily married man then and eager to rejoin his family in Tennessee. He had lived through the harrowing ordeal but a short time later had learned that his family was gone.

Funny how a man's values could be turned upside down in an instant. One minute he'd been desperate to stay alive, the next he'd wondered if living was worthwhile.

On the other hand, look how that adventure had turned out for T. R. Barkley, Matt's older brother. He'd made it through the ordeal, along with the daughter of Mike's commanding officer. Now the two were married and settled in the Green River Valley. And if a half wild scout like T. R. could find a new life in this wilderness, maybe he could, too.

The mare nickered and pulled against the reins. Mike turned eastward and cantered back toward the wagons. Yes, life was worth living, he'd concluded after months of agonized study in the scriptures. As long as God wanted him on this earth, he'd do his best to stay healthy. Right now he had sixty families to worry about.

When he arrived at the wagon train, they were stopped for the nooning hour. Mike headed for the escort's camp for dinner but had to pass a dozen emigrants' wagons to reach it. He came even with the Paines' wagon and started to pass it, then reconsidered. Dorcas was pouring water into the dishpan while Mr. Paine and the children finished their meal. Mike dismounted, tying the mare's reins to the wagon wheel.

"Good day, Mrs. Paine. I thank you for your hospitality last night. That was the best meal I've had for months."

"Oh, go on, Corporal. It was nothing special, and you know it."

He smiled. "You have a touch with venison stew, if I do say so."

"We missed you at the dancing."

"Ah, well, duty." He looked around the camp, mentally ticking off the family members.

As if reading his mind, Dorcas said, "Lydia should have been back by now."

"Oh? And where is she?" It was tantamount to admitting he couldn't make it through a day without a glimpse of Lydia, but suddenly Mike didn't care, and his heart was light.

"She went looking for those mouthwatering burdocks you and Gleason were talking about yesterday."

Mike stood still, a sudden fear striking him. "She went by herself?"

"Yes, we were near the place, Gleason told us an hour or more ago, and she had her teeth set for some. Said she'd catch up by noontime, but. . ."

"But, ma'am, we passed a Sioux camp this morning."

Mr. Paine came and stood beside him. "You think she could have run into trouble?"

"That was hours ago, the Indian camp," Dorcas said, taking away Nathan's empty plate.

"It was three miles back, ma'am. These oxen move slowly." Mike hurried toward his horse.

"I'll go with you," said Paine.

"No need. Most likely she's fine, but if I'm not back in thirty minutes, tell the sergeant."

"Take Beauty," said Paine. "Miss Jackson will need a mount."

eight

Mike waited while Paine threw the saddle on his roan. He would have preferred to bring Lydia back riding with him, the way Gleason had taken her through the river, but he knew the feisty mare wouldn't put up with the weight of them both. If he tied so much as a bedroll behind the saddle, the bay bucked and plunged in fury.

He led Beauty along and trotted both horses through the area where the extra livestock grazed, then cantered a mile along the back trail until he could see the knoll. The burdocks grew on the other side.

Lord, let her be there safe and sound, he prayed as he topped the rise. It was very important to him that Lydia was safe, and he knew it was more than his duty to protect the emigrants that spurred him on. His initial attraction to her had grown into admiration over the weeks since they'd left Fort Laramie. From everything he saw and heard, she was a spirited, hardworking, not to mention lovely, young woman, and whether she wanted to or not, she had stolen his heart. He would hate to see anything happen to her, even though she seemed to have an aversion to him.

Lydia was kneeling on the turf, digging with a large knife. Beside her lay a lumpy burlap sack. Her bonnet hung down her back by its strings, and her mulberry-colored dress was blotched with dirt. Her determined concentration made him smile. She was beautiful even with her nose smudged with grime and the wind tugging strands of hair loose from their pins.

"You'll ruin that blade, using it for a shovel."

She jumped and stared up at him. He dismounted and let both horses' reins trail on the short buffalo grass.

"You!" She stood up, pushing a tendril of hair back with her filthy hand.

"Yes, it's me, herder of stragglers."

"I'm not a straggler. I'm a forager."

"Did you know it's past noon, and the wagons are a mile west of here?"

She swallowed. "Really?"

"Really. The Paines are worried about you."

She flushed slightly and reached for the sack. "I'm sorry. It took longer than I thought to find these. But I don't need you to bring me back like a naughty child."

"Mrs. Paine was afraid those Sioux would be after you."

She waved that aside. "Dorcas worries too much. I'm armed, as you see."

He took a step nearer, perturbed because his heart was leaping. He found her more appealing than ever. It was silly, losing his head over a girl like this, especially one who disliked him. But for all her standoffishness, he knew she had a compassionate heart. He'd seen that when she wanted to protect the Gordon boy. She was clever and diligent and a big help to Dorcas. The Paine children loved her. Mr. and Mrs. Paine respected her. . .and she was beautiful.

"All right, I admit I was worried, too. Those Sioux were cordial this morning when we rode by with thirty armed troopers. They might not be so friendly if they happened on a young woman foolish enough to go wandering around by herself." *Especially one with hair that glints fiery in the sun,* he thought.

She drew herself up, ready to do battle. "I am perfectly capable of taking care of myself."

"That may be, in most situations, but—"

"But what? I'm not smart enough to find my way back to the train?"

A taunt leaped to his lips, but he bit it back. "You're not safe out here alone, and you're causing those kind people some distress. Now, get on the horse." Her face contorted in resentment, and he added belatedly, "Please."

"I can walk, thank you."

Mike knew she was just trying to make him angry because of their past encounters, and maybe he deserved that, although it seemed his men caused an awful lot of bad blood between him and Lydia with their thoughtless remarks. But it was partly his own fault.

"Lydia, a lot of people care about you." That wasn't a brilliant opening, but he was rusty when it came to courtship.

"Oh, really?" She glared at him.

"Yes. You've got them worried sick." He closed the distance between them and stood staring into her glittering blue eyes. She was so lovely! Did he really think she would give him a chance? Probably not. She had already made up her mind about him.

The knowledge that he'd been looking at her as an irresistibly attractive woman for weeks aggravated him. He had tried to resist the feelings that lay dormant so long. But not anymore. He was ready to admit the way she affected him, ready to move on beyond his grief, and ready to pursue a future with her. He swallowed hard. "You could at least have brought Paine's dog with you."

"I don't need a watchdog, four-legged or otherwise."

Her defiance made his adrenaline surge, but Mike buried his impulse to seize her by the shoulders and shake her. No, he realized, he didn't want to shake her. More than anything he wanted to kiss her.

She stood her ground, her blue eyes shining. *I ought to step back,* he thought, though he wanted to get closer. In fact, the urge to sweep her into his arms was almost overwhelming. But no, that type of behavior would confirm all her ideas about him, not to mention the trouble he would be in when Reese got wind of it. He took a slow, careful breath, trying to frame a courteous request for her to mount Paine's horse and ride back to the camp with him.

"You're so beautiful," he whispered, and was appalled that he'd let the thought leave his lips.

Her eyes flared. She clenched her fist on the hilt of the knife. Regret flooded Mike's mind as he realized he'd stepped over an invisible line and frightened her with his intensity.

Before he could launch an apology, she glared at him in contempt. "Is this the way you treat all the ladies in your care?"

"No, miss." Mike cleared his throat, anxious to make amends. "To be truthful, I haven't said such a thing to a woman since— well, since I left my wife in Tennessee."

"Your wife?" Her eyes blazed, and quicker than the mare could shy she slapped him.

Mike watched her ruefully as she strode to the roan, gathered up the reins and mounted, the butcher knife still in her hand. She didn't look at him again but turned the horse toward the wagon train and galloped off, riding low over the saddle.

He sighed, watching her go. A fine hash he'd made of this situation. Before she had merely disliked him. Now she had good reason to hate him. His nebulous hopes of courting her were ruined.

He settled his hat firmly on his head and rubbed his scratchy jaw as he walked toward his mare, carrying the sack of burdock roots. "Well, now, that gal packs a wallop, wouldn't you say, Lady? Perhaps I should have said, my *late* wife."

The bay mare nickered and sidestepped as he pulled the stirrup toward him.

❧

Mr. Paine took Beauty's bridle as Lydia dismounted, looking up at her in anxious silence.

"I'm sorry I was late getting back."

Dorcas stood by the wagon, knotting her apron in her hands. One glance at her sweet, troubled face put Lydia in acute repentance. She walked over to Dorcas and held out the knife. "I didn't intend to cause you any worry, but I can see I stayed away too long, and I wasn't here to help you get dinner."

"Don't worry about that." Dorcas handed her the plate she had reserved for her. "I'm just glad you're in one piece."

"Did you get any burdocks?" Nathan asked.

Lydia clapped her hand to her mouth. "I forgot the sack!" She looked from Mr. Paine to Dorcas. "I could ride back and get it."

Mr. Paine shook his head. "Let's forget about it."

Lydia hesitated, and in that instant Harpy began a joyful barking.

"There's Corporal Brown!" Nathan raced across the grass toward the approaching horse.

Lydia turned her back to the horseman, her color rising. "Dorcas, I apologize for my behavior, but I don't wish to speak to Brown again." She took her plate and ducked behind the wagon.

A moment later she heard Mr. Paine call a hearty greeting to Brown as the hoofbeats came closer and stopped.

"There you go, ma'am," she heard Brown say.

"Bless you! Lydia said she forgot to fetch it." Dorcas sounded her usual cheerful self.

Brown said something else, but Lydia was prevented from understanding it by the noise her teeth made as she ground them. Why couldn't he stay out of her life? He thought it was his duty to provoke her on a regular basis. It was time someone disabused him of that notion.

She set her tin plate on the wagon's lazy board, where tired pedestrians could catch a ride, and took one angry step toward the end of the wagon. Then she stopped. Vivid in her mind was the memory of that exquisite moment when Corporal Michael Brown had looked deep into her eyes and said, *"You're so beautiful."* Only for an instant had she let herself revel in that, imagining what it would be like to be his sweetheart, to let him pull her gently into his embrace and kiss her.

Then she had done what any decent girl would do. But how could she dress him down, remembering how she had hesitated, how she had hated to end that blissful moment?

Her cheeks flamed at the memory, and her heart raced. The corporal was married, and she had enjoyed seeing the light of admiration in his brown eyes. It hit her with terrible force that she had wished for just such a moment. All these weeks, she had insisted to herself that she didn't like him, but that wasn't true. He aggravated her, but part of the aggravation was the knowledge that she could never respond to his advances.

What if she had? What if she had simply lowered her lashes and said, "Thank you?" What would have happened next?

She wished she were free to answer the longing she had witnessed in his eyes and voice. The idea shocked Lydia. Was she wicked to feel this way?

No other man was like Michael Brown, she was sure, although she had never been courted, and no one else had ever held this fascination for her. As much as she told herself she disliked the man, she found herself drawn to him. He was so much more alive and energetic than any other man she had ever known. And even though he professed to be uneducated, there was a depth to his conversation that told her he was well-read and contemplative.

And what did this mean, as far as her future was concerned? She had promised to teach school for a year and could not attach herself to a man, any man, but especially not a married man. Shame washed over her. She had fallen for a married man! It was unthinkable.

"Dear God, forgive me," she whispered. "I didn't know!"

But that was no excuse. Her future was settled. She had promised the school board that she would arrive, single, by October 1 and carry out her duty as teacher at their new academy—an unmarried teacher. That fleeting moment between her and Michael Brown must never be repeated.

No, she couldn't march out there now and berate him. It was as much her fault as his. She sank down on the lazy board in despair.

When she heard Dorcas calling, "Good-bye, Corporal. Thank you!" she walked slowly out from behind the wagon.

"There you are, dear. We've got to put the dinner things away." Dorcas clucked her tongue as she noticed Lydia's plate. "You're not done eating? Hurry up. They'll be pulling out any minute."

"How did you learn to ride so well, Miss Lydia?" Nathan asked, as she sank wearily onto the dish crate.

"Now, Nathan, let her be," said Dorcas.

"It's all right," Lydia told her. She didn't feel like eating, but she put a forkful of cold beans into her mouth, and as soon as Dorcas turned away to put the skillet in the wagon, she held her plate out to Harpy. The dog made short work of her meal. Nathan watched with wide, blue eyes.

"Shh!" Lydia warned him, and he nodded with a con-spiratorial smile, glancing around to be certain his mother didn't see. "My father taught me to ride," Lydia whispered.

"Pa lets me ride Beauty sometimes."

"She's a good horse."

"I'll bet you can ride better 'n my pa."

Lydia smiled. "I don't know about that." It wouldn't do any good to make the boy think less of his father. Mr. Paine might be slow-moving, but he was a kind, thoughtful man. Now, if Nathan had said she rode better than Corporal Brown. . .but that probably wasn't true. She had observed Brown enough to know he was an excellent horseman.

"I rode Bright today," Nathan said, referring to the docile lead ox.

Lydia smiled and stood up. "Before you know it, you'll be driving a team." She hastened to help load up the dishes, determined to forget about the mortifying incident with Corporal Brown.

That afternoon she walked alone. She was too embarrassed to face the Paines again so soon and too introspective to enjoy the company of the other young women. She was afraid if she spoke to anyone, they would read in her expression her confusion and know somehow that she had feelings for Michael Brown.

Gleason found her where she trudged along against the wind. He pulled his mule up beside her.

"Miss Jackson, how are you today?"

She barely glanced at him. "I'm fine."

"Some of the folks are asking if I'll play again this evening, so they can dance."

Lydia shrugged.

"Would you come if I played the fiddle?"

"I don't know. Maybe."

The mule walked beside her, and after a few seconds, Gleason said bleakly, "Well, so long. Maybe I'll see you tonight."

An hour later Dorcas came toward her, carrying little Jenny.

"Lydia, come ride for a while, dear. Please." Her face was creased with anxiety, and Lydia gave in, following her back to the wagon.

When they were settled on the seat, Dorcas laid Jenny on the pile of bedding just inside the wagon cover.

"Trooper Gleason stopped by earlier. He asked me if you were all right."

Lydia nodded wearily. "I saw him."

"He's quite taken with you," Dorcas said.

Lydia shrugged. "I'm not interested."

Dorcas smiled. "I knew it! Corporal Brown is perfect for you. You needn't have been so coy when you came back this noon."

"Coy?" Lydia said dully.

"Well, yes. I mean, if you love him—"

"*Love him?*" Lydia stared at her hostess. "Love Michael Brown? That's impossible."

Dorcas smiled. "And why would you say that? He thinks highly of you."

"Well, I cannot stand the sight of him."

Dorcas's eyebrows arched in surprise. "It didn't seem that way when you came tearing in on Beauty, with your cheeks flushed and your eyes all dreamy."

"Please, Dorcas! He's married!" The words nearly choked her, and she was surprised that Dorcas didn't react with shock.

Instead, Dorcas touched her sleeve and said tenderly, "Don't you know?"

"Know what?"

"Oh, my. No wonder you think so badly of him. Lydia, dear, the man's a widower."

Lydia stared at her companion. "Are you sure?"

"Absolutely. He's been out here with the army away from his family for years. He was all set to go back East when word came last year—or was it the year before?—that his wife had died. Poor man. He was distraught. They say he rode out on the prairie alone for two days, then went back to Fort Bridger and reenlisted. Couldn't stand to go back to Virginia—"

"Tennessee," Lydia murmured.

"Yes, Tennessee." Dorcas nodded. "You're always correct, dear. Anyway, he decided he'd rather stay out here and keep soldiering than go back and face the emptiness of his old home without his dear wife and little son."

"There was a child, too? How very sad!" Lydia tried to fit the tragic tale with what she already knew, or thought she knew, about Michael Brown. It changed everything, and she wasn't sure she could adjust her image of him so quickly. She cleared her throat. "And how did you learn all this?"

"I wouldn't gossip, of course," Dorcas assured her, "but Mrs. Miller's husband told her, and he had it from one of the troopers." She looked primly at Lydia from the corner of her eye.

Lydia cringed inwardly. Dorcas definitely ran her tongue too much, if in a genteel way. She straightened and gathered her skirts. "I think I'll hop down and walk some more."

Dorcas grasped her arm. "I'm certain he cares about you. Don't you care?"

She sighed. "All that about Corporal Brown is very sad, but if it's true, he would probably prefer not to become an object of pity in the train."

"Pity?" Dorcas stared at her in alarm. "Michael Brown is not a man to pity! He's a fine fellow, and he's a born leader. The troopers all love him. I expect he's one of those rare men who will work his way up through the ranks and come out a general."

Lydia smiled at the thought. "General Brown. Perhaps he will. Dorcas, would you mind if I stretch out inside with Jenny for a while? I find I'm very tired, after all."

"Of course you can! A little rest will do you good."

Lydia crawled into the shadowy interior of the wagon. It was piled high with the family's belongings, and she settled herself carefully on top of the luggage and quilts. If anything, it was hotter in the wagon than out in the full sun, and she couldn't get comfortable on her makeshift bed. She lay on her side, watching Jenny sleep.

Her guilt grew as she went over what Dorcas had told her. If it were true, if Michael Brown were really a widower, then it was no sin for him to pursue a young woman like herself. Was he trying to court her? Or was it just a lark for him? She hadn't supposed he took anything too seriously except the danger brought on by nature and the travelers' carelessness. But if he were free, and if he were indeed attempting to court her, that changed everything. Corporal Brown had done nothing wrong.

She, on the other hand, had allowed herself to develop an admiration for him while she was pledged to fulfill a year's contract. Tears rolled down her face. She wriggled to the back of the wagon and opened her carpetbag. From deep in the bottom, she pulled out the contract and unfolded it.

Her signature and that of the school board chairman stared up at her. There was no changing it. The document had meant so much to her when she received it. It was the beginning of a new life, and it renewed her optimism. It was more than the answer to her sudden poverty and homelessness after her aunt died. It was a chance to launch an innovative school and touch many lives. She had been sure it was God's purpose for her. Had anything changed? Surely God would not want her to go back on her word just because a man was interested in her. That was one thing her father had taught her—never break your word.

She held the paper to her heart, the tears flowing freely now. *Lord, forgive me. I've made a promise, and I intend to keep it. I don't mean to feel these things for Michael Brown. I don't want to feel them. I want to fulfill my contract. Help me, Father.* She collapsed with her arms on Mr. Paine's toolbox and wept.

At last she straightened and wiped her eyes, tucking the envelope into the pocket of her dress. If she carried it around with her, it would be a constant reminder of her duty and her promise. She mustn't let her obstinate heart run away with her again. Even if Michael was eligible, she could not, would not, even for a moment think of the possibility. And she must never allow herself to be alone with him again.

Dorcas's words came back to her. *"If you love him—"*

"I don't, Lord," she whispered brokenly. "I can't love him. I won't." She hopped down over the tailboard and walked out onto the prairie, then kept pace with the ox team as the words cycled over and over in her mind. "I don't love him."

nine

It was early when they stopped that evening close to Independence Rock. A holiday atmosphere ran through the camp. Women hastened to do a quick wash and a large baking. Young people scrambled up the rock to view the plain from above.

Lydia helped Dorcas wash the children's clothing. The hard work took her mind off her inner struggles, and she plunged into it gladly. She was spreading the wet, clean clothes to dry when Frances Bailey arrived, breathless.

"Lydia! Mr. Miller says we'll stay over for a day of rest. We're making good time, and there's enough grass for the cattle here."

"Joy!" Dorcas cried. "I want to repack the supplies tomorrow. We've got the children's clothes washed, Lydia. Perhaps tomorrow we can do a load for us old folks."

"Wonderful," Lydia agreed. They seldom had time to do a complete laundry job along the way.

"Some are talking about walking over to Devil's Gate tomorrow morning," Frances said.

Lydia shaded her eyes against the sun and squinted westward. The tall cliffs that squeezed the river between them stood a couple of miles away. The cleft in the hills was like a jagged knife cut in a loaf of bread. The wagons wouldn't go through Devil's Gate, as there wasn't enough space between the cliffs and the river for a road, but some folks were eager to get a closer look at the landmark.

"I'll go," Lydia said. "After I help Mrs. Paine with the washing."

"That's capital. I'll tell my mother you're going. Then she'll know I'll be safe." Frances was quite pretty when she smiled,

Lydia realized. If she weren't so shy, the men would flock around her.

"Did you dance last evening?" she asked. "I didn't see you."

Frances flushed slightly. "I did. It was early on."

"Be we allowed to ask with whom?" Dorcas asked, her eyes twinkling.

"Well, I took a turn with Charlie Sawyer, but that was no fun. He was fuming because Ellen was carrying on so with that soldier."

"And then?" Dorcas prodded.

Frances didn't seem to mind Dorcas's questioning. "Well, Charlie's friend Tim Anderson asked me next."

Her color deepened, and Lydia wondered if Frances wasn't enamored of Tim Anderson. She knew the boy by sight. He was good-looking but quiet, and he had lost three fingers from his left hand in an accident when he was little. Dorcas had detailed the story to her shortly after they'd left Fort Laramie. Lydia had thought Tim and Charlie were an odd pair. Charlie was constantly calling attention to himself, while Tim was content to remain in the background. The girls seemed to skip right over Tim when cataloging the eligible young men in the company.

"That must have been a highlight of the evening's program," Dorcas said, and Frances's blush went crimson.

"It was. . .very nice." She didn't look at either of them.

"But I looked for you after Mrs. Paine took Jenny," Lydia protested. "I saw Tim and Charlie, but not you."

Frances sighed. "By the time my dance with Tim was finished, Charlie was upset. He started saying vile things about Trooper Stedman. It was very embarrassing. I could see Tim was angry with Charlie for talking that way in front of me, and so I excused myself."

"I'm sure there were plenty of other fellows who would have been happy to dance with you," Dorcas said.

Frances smiled. "I didn't mind."

No, Lydia thought, *you didn't mind a bit. You'd had one magical*

*moment with Tim, and you didn't want to spoil it by dancing with
some oaf of a trooper afterward.*

She smiled at Frances. "I'm glad you had a nice time."

Frances had a look of utter contentment, and Lydia felt a stab
of envy. Would she have felt that way if Corporal Brown had
come along and asked her to dance? She knew she wouldn't.
Instead, she'd have been in worse turmoil than she was now.

"I'll come by for you in the morning, after I've helped
Mother with the chores," Frances said.

"You girls can take a lunch and have a picnic party," Dorcas
said.

Lydia laughed. "That's very sweet. Thank you."

She thought of staying away from the dancing that evening,
but she couldn't see much point in that. There were so many
soldiers along, it seemed almost a patriotic obligation to give
an hour or two to dancing with them. Besides, if she hid out
during the festivities, the other women would think it strange.
Margaret Sawyer certainly would make cutting remarks about
her absence the next day.

After supper Lydia tried to coax the wrinkles from her
blue dress with a damp cloth. She'd been keeping the dress in
reserve for when the others became too shabby, and it was full
of wrinkles from resting in the bottom of her carpetbag.

A sudden thought struck her, and she called, "Dorcas, do
you think it would be all right for me to lend one of my dresses
to Minnie Carver?"

Dorcas looked up from her mending. "That would be most
thoughtful of you. Then she and her sister could both enjoy
the dancing. Of course, you'd have to be careful how you
phrased your offer."

Lydia nodded. "Yes, I wouldn't want to offend her."

Dorcas bent over the button she was reattaching to her best
dress. "I thought of it last night, but those girls are far and
away slimmer than I am. They could never fit into one of my
dresses."

Lydia frowned. "Don't belittle yourself, Dorcas. I think you are the perfect size, and Mr. Paine does, too."

"Mr. Paine does what?" her host boomed, and Lydia jumped.

"There now, you shouldn't startle her so," Dorcas chided.

Lydia laughed. "I didn't know you were there, sir. Your wife and I were just discussing a matter that is better left unspoken in mixed company."

He chuckled. "Well then, I shan't ask again. Trooper Gleason is tuning his fiddle. Will you be dancing with me tonight, Mrs. Paine?"

"With none other," Dorcas replied. She stuck her needle into her pincushion and stood. "Lydia, if you're going to perform that errand of mercy we spoke of, you'd best be quick."

"I'll be back in time to watch the children while you and Mr. Paine have the first dance." Lydia grabbed the blue dress and hurried toward the Carvers' wagon.

Once again, Michael Brown was absent from the clearing while the music filled the air. After Mr. and Mrs. Paine relieved her from baby tending, Lydia danced and smiled and laughed at several dozen jokes. She gave out minimal information about herself and urged the troopers and farmers to tell her about themselves, and all seemed eager to comply.

She glimpsed Frances once, dancing starry-eyed with Tim Anderson. Margaret Sawyer was rarely without a partner. Lydia saw Charlie Sawyer dancing with anyone but Ellen Hadley, and once she saw Ellen with Trooper Stedman. John Gleason tried to catch Lydia's eye. She gave him what she hoped was an impartial smile and began to wish she were elsewhere. The trooper she was dancing with now, Wilson, was excessively attentive, and as soon as the melody came to an end, she thanked him briefly and slipped away toward the Paines' wagon.

She almost collided with Pete Stedman and Ellen Hadley in the shadows between the wagons.

"Oh, I'm sorry."

"It's all right," Stedman said.

"Oh, Lydia," Ellen stammered.

Lydia swallowed hard, wondering if she'd interrupted an intimate moment.

"Lovely night," Stedman said in the awkward silence.

"Yes."

"Did you see Minnie Carver?" Ellen asked. "She found a new dress somewhere."

"Yes, I saw her. She looks lovely in it," Lydia said with a secret smile.

"It's her color," Ellen agreed. "But if she had it all this time, why didn't she wear it last night? Well, good evening, Lydia." She grasped the trooper's hand and tugged him toward the circle of dancers.

Mr. and Mrs. Paine were sitting together on a quilt beside their wagon, holding hands.

Lydia smiled at them. "Thank you for letting me go. It's not too late for you folks to have another dance together."

"What, you're all done?" Mr. Paine said.

Dorcas chuckled. "Perhaps the right partner wasn't there this evening."

"Some men just don't like to dance." Mr. Paine scratched his head. "Of course, some of the troopers nearly came to blows earlier, fighting over who was *not* going to have sentry duty."

"The married men should stand guard and let the bachelors have a chance to socialize," Dorcas said. "It only makes sense."

"Well, I don't know. Sergeant Reese told me he doesn't like to see the men get attached to our young ladies. It can cause trouble later on, you know."

"How is that?" Dorcas asked.

Mr. Paine hesitated and looked at Lydia, then murmured, "Mixed company, m' dear."

"Not for long," Lydia assured him. "My feet are tired, and I'm retiring. Do go and have another round."

"It's more peaceful here," Dorcas said a bit wistfully.

Lydia supposed the phlegmatic couple had had enough excitement for one evening, but as she climbed into the back of the wagon to grope for her carpetbag, she heard Mr. Paine say softly, "Perhaps a walk in the moonlight."

"Lovely," Dorcas said, "but not too far from the wagons. The sergeant is adamant about folks wandering off at night."

When Lydia descended with her bedroll, the Paines were gone. She settled down next to Jenny and Nathan. The music had mellowed from the rollicking square dances to a dreamy waltz, a sign that Gleason would stop playing soon.

She sent up an abbreviated prayer of thanks, knowing she couldn't stay awake much longer. The exertion of the day coupled with her emotional upheaval over Corporal Brown left her exhausted.

The stars glittered above her in the purple-black sky. She'd never learned much about the stars. Science seemed to be one area Miss Clarkson had neglected. They shone bright, tantalizingly close. She wondered if Michael could see the same stars. Could he hear the music? And was he thinking about her? She couldn't make herself wish that he wasn't.

ten

It was nearly a week before Lydia worked up her courage to set things right with Michael. They toiled along the Sweetwater, climbing slowly toward South Pass, and every mile was a struggle. The road going down the other side was even worse. There was less time for socializing, and everyone was too tired to do more than attend to the basic needs of food, fuel, and water.

Lydia watched Michael guardedly, all the while feeling guilty, but she saw no private opportunity to speak with the busy corporal. Her mortification increased as she pondered all that had passed between them. She came to the conclusion that she had been wrong to strike him and that she must express her regret to him, but she was afraid. Of what? Afraid of his disdain? She had scorned him. Afraid of his rejection? She had rebuffed him. She knew she needed to seek his forgiveness regardless of his reaction. Over and over she poured out her heart to God, pleading for the strength to do what was right.

The young women on the train were swooning over Corporal Brown. His tragic tale had leaked out, and the ladies romanticized his plight.

The mothers of marriageable daughters envisioned snagging a handsome, hardworking noncommissioned officer as a son-in-law, and Brown was rumored to have a supper invitation at a different campfire each evening, but Lydia saw him ride in after dusk more often than not and shuffle slowly to the army cook wagon after putting his horse up.

The girls looked for excuses to speak to him and shamelessly sought for him on the one evening since Independence Rock when there was dancing, but somehow Michael seemed to have been assigned picket duty again that evening.

But one night he approached their campfire with Mr. Paine, and Lydia fought the impulse to pay a hasty call on the Baileys. She knew it was past time she faced him. The opportunity came when Dorcas asked her to fetch a skillet Mrs. Williams had borrowed at the noon stop.

"I'd be happy to escort you, Miss Jackson," Michael said. It was what she wanted—a chance to speak to him.

She walked woodenly beside him, wondering how to broach the subject. The Williams' wagon was only four spots away from the Paines', and the walk was a short one. They were halfway before she slowed and faced him with determination.

"Corporal Brown, please forgive me for my behavior last week. It was uncalled for, and I wish you would excuse it."

He stopped walking. A smile played at his lips.

"And what behavior is that, Miss Jackson?"

She felt irritation rising. "You know very well what I'm talking about. I mean, when you—you rode out after me." She knew her face was scarlet, and she turned hastily away, heading for the Williams' camp.

"Oh, you mean when you went off alone in Indian territory and I came to fetch you back, and I told you how beautiful you looked, and you—"

"Hush!" She rounded on him furiously, looking around to be sure no one had overheard.

He laughed. "As far as I'm concerned, Miss Jackson, there's nothing to forgive on that score. If anything, I should be the one seeking absolution."

"I. . .disagree."

"Seems we do a lot of that."

She gritted her teeth. "Fine. I've apologized for my behavior. If you won't accept that, I can't do anything more."

His smile was dazzling in the dusk. "I understand. 'She hath done what she could.'"

Lydia's ire rose once more. Why must he tease her? Why couldn't he just be nice for once? "You needn't rebuke me in that supercilious manner, as if I were an uppity prig." She turned again in a whirl of skirts, but he seized her wrist and held her immobile.

"Whoa there, Miss—what did you call yourself? An uppish twig? If you can quote the dictionary at me, why can't I refute you with scripture?"

He was still laughing, she could see, and suddenly she felt very small and vain. "That was scripture?"

"Yes, but I shouldn't have tossed it out so lightly. Scripture's not meant to be trifled with."

Lydia gulped. "I–I'm sorry, Corporal. Truly."

"It's Mike."

"No, it's not. It can't be."

"Why not?" His voice was almost tender now, and when she glanced up, his melting brown eyes seared her conscience.

"I—I can't be more than friends with you."

He was quiet for an instant, then said softly, "Are we friends now? I couldn't tell."

She sobbed, and he released her wrist, bending to look closely at her, full of concern. "Miss—Lydia, I'm sorry. I shouldn't bait you, but you must know you're lovely when you're angry."

"No," she choked. "Don't say things like that. You make me—"

"What?"

She shrugged helplessly. He looked around and then pulled her quickly between two wagons, over the tongue of the Carvers' wagon, and a few steps out onto the darkening prairie.

"What is it, Lydia? Something's got you all worked up."

She stood trembling, trying to keep back the tears. She would not cry in front of him. It would give him too much satisfaction to know she had shed tears over him.

"It's just that the way you talk to me—"

"I admire you, Lydia. I don't mean to upset you."

"But you do. If you're attempting to make advances toward me, you have to stop," she choked.

"My intentions are honorable. Isn't it obvious that I'm wildly attracted to you?"

She looked away helplessly. "And you expect me to believe

that? At first I thought you despised me."

"No, never that."

"And now. . .well, now I suppose you find pursuing me a diversion."

"Lydia, I've admired you from the first day I met you. But you seemed remote, beyond my grasp. I've teased you because I didn't think you'd look twice at me. If you'll let me, I'd like to court you in earnest." She felt his fingers rest lightly on her sleeve, and she stepped back.

"Don't, please."

He nodded. "You can't be more than friends."

"That's right."

Mike frowned. "You must know by now that my wife is. . . deceased."

"Yes, I heard, and I'm sorry I thought so badly of you. I should have known you wouldn't do such a thing."

"How could you know it? I'm the churlish type."

She hid her face with one hand, wishing she had never begun the conversation. After a moment she cleared her throat and looked up at him. He was watching her intently. "Mr. Paine thinks highly of you. He says that you're loyal. That tells me, by implication, that you wouldn't desert your wife or seek other female company if she were living. Mr. Paine wouldn't like you if you were that type of man."

He nodded slowly. "Mr. Paine is wiser than most give him credit for."

"Yes."

"For instance, he wouldn't lend you his horse the time you—"

"Let's not get into that," she said hastily. "I think we've established the fact that I misjudged you. I'm very sorry I. . . struck you. And I would like to be your friend, as the Paines are your friends, but that must be the sum of it, Corporal."

"Michael," he said softly.

"Michael." He held her gaze, and she felt an overwhelming desire once more to be in his arms, to have a man like that care for her so fiercely that it wouldn't bother her in the least when he laughed at some little absurdity, because she was secure in knowing he would love her always.

"Mr. Paine is right, Lydia. I'm not the type to toy with a woman's affections. I'm sorry that I made you uncomfortable. What I really wanted was to win your heart, but I could see that I hadn't much chance. Tell me I was wrong."

She made herself look away from his eyes. "Michael, I have a contract. I cannot break it."

There. It was out. She glanced up at him, and a deep sadness had settled over his features.

"I see."

She pulled in a shaky breath. "I have to get the skillet back to Dorcas."

"Of course." He touched her elbow and led her back to the slight gap between the wagons. Mr. Carver was about to close it by piling sacks of feed and household goods about the wagon tongue.

"Oh, Corporal Brown. Didn't see you there."

Michael stepped into the enclosure and held out his hand to help Lydia over the barrier. Carver raised his eyebrows. "Miss Jackson."

"Mr. Carver."

Minnie Carver's curious face appeared in the opening behind the wagon seat.

Michael touched his hat brim and walked on toward the Williams' wagon, still holding Lydia's hand. *Oh, dear, there'll be gossip in camp tonight,* she thought, but she savored the brief moment, only pulling her hand away when they came to the Williams' campfire. *I'll never touch him again,* she thought sadly.

On the way back, he carried the cast-iron skillet, and Lydia marched along with him, hastening because she knew Dorcas was waiting.

"It's ironic," she said when they were nearly there. "All the girls in the company will be heartbroken when they hear that you were out walking with me, but there's nothing to it."

He smiled. "I'm sure they'll figure that out in a few days, when they see how you avoid me."

"I shan't try to avoid you anymore, so long as you understand my position."

"I don't fully understand it, but I respect your wishes."

"Thank you."

She went to help Dorcas with supper, leaving him to resume his conversation with Mr. Paine, who was cleaning his rifle.

Lydia picked up the water bucket and looked around for Nathan. They were camped close to the river tonight, and there was no need for a guard when she went for water.

"Let me get that," Michael said, reaching for the bucket.

Lydia eyed him in surprise. "I can get it."

"The corporal and I will give you a recess this evening," Mr. Paine said, rising and setting his rifle aside.

Michael grinned. "That's right. Give us all your buckets while you have the chance, ladies."

Dorcas quickly gave them the three pails she could lay hands on, and the men struck out for the water with Nathan tagging along.

"You know my opinion," said Dorcas, looking pointedly at Lydia.

"Yes, ma'am, I do." Lydia smiled. She knew Dorcas couldn't refrain from voicing it again, anyway.

"That," said Dorcas, "is a very nice young man."

eleven

Mike took Pete Stedman with him on scout duty. The corporal had been over this trail many times. He didn't expect any problems in this area, though the trail was steep in places. They'd make it past the mail relay station today and within days would reach the cutoff that would take them north into the Oregon Territory.

"You keep clear of Charlie Sawyer," Mike told him as they rode along.

Stedman nodded. "The sergeant read me those lines a week ago."

"Yes, well, he's serious. The wagon master told him yesterday that one of the boys heard Charlie threatening to kill you if you didn't stop seeing the Hadley girl. It doesn't take much for a lovesick young man to lose it out here."

Stedman grimaced. "It wasn't my intention to stir up trouble, Corporal."

Mike shook his head. "Then what was your intention? I can't see any good way for this to end."

"I care about Ellen."

"She's too young to be an army wife. What could you offer her? Best end it and let her go on with her family."

Stedman was silent, and Mike left him to his thoughts.

A Pony Express rider galloped past them when the two scouts were only a couple of miles out from the relay station. He waved, but as Mike expected, he didn't stop to talk.

"Let's go as far as the Pony station and see if we can pick up any news," Mike suggested.

"Sure," said Pete.

They went at a much more leisurely pace than the mail carrier, and by the time they reached the small outpost, the rider had passed his mail pouch to the young man heading out for Fort Bridger and was eating his dinner.

"You got Sergeant Reese with you on that emigrant train?" he asked, eyeing the yellow chevrons on Mike's sleeves.

"Yes, we do," Mike said.

The boy grinned. "Tell him Mrs. Sergeant Reese says, 'It's a boy.' She didn't have enough money for a letter, but the fellows told her we'd pass the word along until we either caught up with his wagon train or hit Bridger. I'd have stopped to tell him, but we're not supposed to, and I knew it would take too long to locate him. Folks always want you to stop and gab. Can't do that in this business."

Mike was glad he had some good news to share for a change. It would lift the spirits of everyone on the wagon train.

Dan Reese whooped when he heard the news. "Get your fiddle out tonight, Jack!" The troopers poked fun at him good-naturedly all evening and took to calling him "Pappy."

Mike spent an hour at the Paines' fireside before he took the evening watch. It was the nearest thing to a home he had visited in months, and he would gladly have spent more time with the family.

"They had a newspaper at the relay station. Congress has approved funding for the transcontinental telegraph line they've been talking about," Mike said.

Mr. Paine shook his head. "Won't be long before folks can go clear to Oregon by stagecoach."

"Railroad," Mike corrected him. "I don't see many more years for this type of wagon train."

"What will the escort do?" Nathan asked.

"You'll be out of work," Mr. Paine said with a smile.

"I expect they'll find us another detail."

"Fighting Injuns?" Nathan asked.

"Could be," Mike said. "There's a lot of war rhetoric back East right now, though. Might be other worries than Indians, as far as the government's concerned."

"You wouldn't fight against Southerners, would you?" Mr. Paine asked, frowning.

Mike inhaled slowly. "I don't know."

"You're a United States Army man," Dorcas said indignantly. "Don't tell me you'd fight against your own country."

Mike stared at the fire, thinking about that.

"Let's hope it doesn't come to that," Mr. Paine said.

Dorcas shook her head. "I'm glad we're out here. If there's going to be fighting in Massachusetts, I don't want to hear about it."

Mike sneaked a look toward where Lydia sat by the rear wheel of the wagon. She was busy with some needlework, taking advantage of the fading light. He hadn't spoken to her once, but he knew she was listening to every word he said to the Paines. She seemed to be making intricate lace out of common cotton string, yards and yards of it.

Music came to them across the camp, and Lydia smiled as she bent over her tatting shuttle. Mike smiled, too, as he recognized the tune. John Gleason was playing "Rock-a-Bye, Baby."

He stood up. "I'd best get to my duty."

"You were in the saddle all day," Mr. Paine said. "Can't you have a whirl with the ladies?"

"Oh, I'm not much of a dancer," Mike replied. "They won't dance long tonight, anyway. Folks are all wrung out from the heat and the terrain we've been wrestling."

"Come by again, now," Dorcas said.

"Thank you, ma'am. Mr. Paine." He glanced toward Lydia. She looked up for a moment and met his gaze for the first time that evening. "Miss Jackson," he said softly with a nod, then turned and walked away.

❧

Mike rode leisurely back toward the wagon train, his chestnut gelding trotting placidly beside Josiah Paine's roan. They'd had a successful day of hunting in the foothills, and a pronghorn was draped over the rump of Mike's horse. Four grouse dangled from Paine's saddle. Mike was feeling content.

"I'll give Dorcas a couple of these birds, and you take the rest to your cook," Paine said.

Mike shook his head. "No, you'll have some venison, too, Josiah. You earned it."

"We're close to the cutoff, aren't we?"

Mike nodded. "Tomorrow or the next day we'll head off north."

"Toward Fort Hall?"

"Well, yes, but they don't use Fort Hall anymore. There's talk of building a new camp, but the army doesn't have an official presence there."

"What are the natives like?"

"The Snake Indians are generally all right. We could run into some hostile Blackfoot, but I doubt it. It's a lot better than this area, with the Sioux. Still, I'll probably be out scouting most of the time once we get through the worst of the mountains."

Paine accepted that without comment. The more time he spent with him, the more Mike liked him. Josiah Paine was a deliberate man, but he was staunch. Mike decided to take a chance. "You've had Miss Jackson with you more than a month now. What do you think of her?"

Josiah looked off toward the river for several seconds, and Mike almost wished he hadn't spoken. But Paine didn't laugh the way Dan Reese would, and he didn't smirk the way Wilson did when women were the topic of conversation. And John Gleason would surely get angry if he hinted that he was interested in Lydia, Mike knew.

Paine scanned the horizon. "She's one of the family now."

Mike nodded, waiting for more.

At last Paine rewarded him. "She's a mite high-strung, but she's good for Dorcas."

"She says she doesn't hate me anymore, but I don't know. She's mighty cool. Is it an act?"

"Hard to say."

Mike swallowed. "She told me the other night she wouldn't avoid me anymore and we'd be friends, but she still doesn't seem to relish my company." The chestnut reached out to nip Beauty's neck, and Mike slapped him on the withers. "Quit that, mister!"

"She's got something pulling her, up ahead in Oregon." Paine's frank, gray eyes invited Mike to give his opinion.

"She said she's party to a contract," Mike said slowly.

"I don't know anything about that."

"I make that out to mean. . .well, do you think it's a marriage contract?"

Paine sniffed and looked at him. "Seems like she'd tell Dorcas that."

Mike nodded, feeling only marginally better. "Could be a business contract, I guess."

"She aims to be a schoolteacher, you know. Bide your time, Mike. That's my advice."

"Guess I don't have much choice. Still, I wonder if there's a gent waiting for her out there."

"Could be, I suppose."

Mike smiled. "You know, I seem to recollect that courtship was a whole lot easier in Tennessee."

"No," Paine replied, "it's not where you are, Mike. They say the older you get, the harder it is."

The wagons were in sight now, and dusk was falling fast. They rode up to the camp and around to the gap that was the gate, then went straight to the Paines' wagon. Dorcas was working over her fire, and Jenny was playing nearby with a rag doll.

"Ah, you brought some meat in." Dorcas's face lit up as her husband dismounted. Paine nodded and began unfastening the thongs that held the birds to the saddle.

"I'll take this antelope to our cook and have him send you a haunch, ma'am," Mike said.

"Thank you. That will be wonderful, Corporal Brown."

Paine handed him two of the grouse. "Come back for supper, now."

Mike darted a glance toward Dorcas, and she smiled at him.

"Of course you will," she said.

"Where's Nathan?" Paine asked, looking around the encampment.

"He and Lydia went for blackberries. They're ripe down in the river bottom, and she begged to go for some."

Paine frowned. "It's nearly dark, Mrs. Paine."

Mike stiffened. Hadn't they learned anything from the burdock incident?

"They took the dog with them," Dorcas said plaintively, but her lower lip trembled.

"Well, that's something," Paine said. "All the same, I think I'll go fetch them. Where did you say?"

"Just downstream a bit from the watering place."

"I'll go with you." Mike quickly dismounted and untied the rawhide strips holding the pronghorn against the cantle of the saddle. "Mind if I leave this meat here for a few minutes, ma'am?"

"N—no," Dorcas said. She picked Jenny up, holding her close to her chest. "I thought they'd be all right, Mr. Paine."

Paine had one foot in the stirrup, but he put it down again and turned toward her. Mike turned away and mounted the gelding he called Sam, but he heard Paine say softly, "Don't worry, missus. I'll bring them back."

They trotted toward the river. The twilight was deep as they rode down toward the willows by the water. Heading eastward, they soon saw the dark bulk of bushes ahead.

"Nathan," Paine called, and they listened.

"Miss Jackson!" Mike yelled, louder. Only the breeze stirring the branches answered.

Paine put his fingers to his lips and let out an ear-piercing whistle that Mike had heard him use before to call his dog, but there was no response.

"I don't like this." Paine looked at him, and Mike nodded.

"Come on." Mike pushed Sam forward toward the berry patch and squinted in the failing light for footprints, broken twigs, bushes that had been stripped of their fruit—any sign that Nathan and Lydia had passed that way.

A faint but definite track ran among the laden bushes, and he forced the horse through the brambles, then pulled up short. Paine's red-brown dog lay still on the ground, a dark stain spreading from his neck. Mike caught his breath and sent up a quick silent prayer. He'd need all the guidance, wit, and courage he could get.

Paine came up beside him and reined in Beauty. He grimaced. "Come on."

Mike fell in behind him. Paine had the right to lead now, and Mike admired him for his coolness. He didn't waste time swearing or climbing down to examine the dog. They went a few paces; then the roan stopped abruptly.

"There," said Paine.

This time Mike dismounted. A small pail lay on the turf, a quart of blackberries spilling from it. He bent to see the ground better, discerning shoe prints and gouges in the soft earth. "They had a bit of a scuffle." He pushed onward and soon found the hoofprints of several unshod horses behind a thicket.

"They waited here. Figured they might get something. Or maybe they were just waiting for dark when they could slip in and try for a few horses." Mike straightened. "Best get more men."

"No, it's late," Paine said. "They might be just minutes ahead of us. Mike, they've got my boy. They say they don't like to trade children back. They'll raise him wild like one of their own. And who knows what they'll do to Lydia. Every minute counts."

Mike looked back uneasily. If they didn't go back to the wagons soon, Dorcas would raise an alarm. Dan Reese would eventually follow.

"Leave a sign for the sergeant," Paine said.

"All right. Let's go." Mike pulled a handkerchief from the pocket of his blue uniform trousers and dropped it a few paces along to mark the faint trail. "They're heading northeast. Probably for that big village Wilson saw yesterday on his scouting duty."

It was difficult to follow the signs in the growing darkness, and he considered ignoring the faint trail and heading Sam at a gallop in a straight line toward the Sioux encampment Wilson had described. He was about to suggest as much when he spotted an item in the short grass. He swung down to retrieve it.

"It's Nathan's shoe," Paine said. He turned it over and looked at the worn sole, shaking his head. "The boy needs new shoes."

Mike decided not to discount the tracks, and they rode without speaking for half an hour.

"How long you figure before we get there?" Paine asked at last.

"Well, their camp was at least twenty miles from our camp, maybe more. That's assuming this party is heading there. I don't know. It seems like we're going more north than we ought if they're headed for the village."

"What does that mean?"

Mike shrugged. "Could mean Wilson was off on his calculations, or it could mean they're not heading there."

"Where, then?"

"Who knows? There are hills up ahead. Could be a band is camped up there. Or they could be from farther away, just out on a raiding spree. They could have a war lodge in the hills."

They rode on under the white slice of moon. Mike wondered what to do if they found that the raiding party had reached the village. The two of them couldn't just storm in there and demand the return of the captives.

The broken terrain slowed them, and Mike let Sam pick his pace as the footing allowed. They approached a stream, and while Paine let Beauty drink, Mike scouted along the bank eastward. When he saw what he was looking for, sixty yards downstream, he gave a low whistle. Paine led his gelding toward him.

"They crossed here," Mike said. The hoofprints close to the stream looked fresh, with water seeping into them.

They forded the stream, and Mike picked out a trail of bent grass in the moonlight. He was so intent on following it that he didn't notice anything else until Paine rode up close to him and hissed. He immediately pulled Sam in and listened. There were definitely soft hoofbeats ahead.

He looked out over the prairie northward and saw irregular rock formations in the distance.

"They're not going to the village," Mike said. "They're heading for those rocks and hills."

"Do you think they know we're here?" Josiah asked.

"Maybe."

"What do you suggest?"

Mike frowned. His impulse was to spur the chestnut and race to catch up with the band of Sioux, but Paine's steadiness in itself was a moderating force. "I don't think there's all that many of them," he said at last. "I've tried to work it out. There's four ponies, at least, but I doubt there's more than six of them."

Paine said nothing, and Mike knew he was waiting for his decision and would follow him without question.

"You primed and loaded?"

Paine drew his rifle from the scabbard. "You said it."

Mike nodded. "Let's catch up but keep quiet if we can. Could be they haven't caught on to us following yet. The closer we can get before they know, the better."

"Right." Paine's eyes gleamed in the faint light. "If I don't make it, you tell Dorcas I did everything I could to get the boy back."

The thought appalled Mike. When the troopers went into combat, it was normal for them to give final instructions to their closest buddies. But Paine. He couldn't imagine going back to the wagon train without him and breaking the news to Dorcas.

"I will." A thought flitted through his mind to give Paine a final message for Lydia, but he couldn't think what to say. *Tell her I'm sorry.* For what? *Tell her I loved her.* That would only distress her. Maybe they should wait for Sergeant Reese to bring the company of troopers up. But no, the Sioux would get away if they didn't strike soon. He lifted the reins and urged Sam forward.

twelve

Lydia clung to the sturdy mustang's saddle. They had ridden for nearly an hour, and she couldn't sustain terror that long. A slow, hot fury rose from deep in her heart. The horses pounded over the turf, through tall grass and wiry brush, up and down over the knolls and swells in the land.

She was used to the faint light of the moon now and could see the other horses running, one ahead of her and one on either side. She knew there was one more behind. The rider to her left held Nathan in front of him.

It was an uncomfortable position. Her captor had somewhere obtained a light cavalry saddle—probably stolen. She would have been much more at ease riding behind the Indian, but she supposed he didn't trust her and assumed she would try to escape. Which she would.

If it weren't for Nathan, that is. She couldn't leave the boy alone on this horrifying journey.

She doubted they would hurt Nathan, but she couldn't be sure. Wild stories had flown from time to time through the wagon train. Michael hadn't seemed unduly worried about the natives, but he'd also been cautious and insisted the women and children not wander off alone, as she had that fateful day when she'd hunted burdocks.

It was tiresome, being tied always to the wagon train and the same people day after day, much as she liked the Paines. When they'd gone for water that afternoon and Nathan had spotted the tempting blackberries, she had immediately begun trying to convince Dorcas that she and the boy would be safe if they took the dog with them. Dorcas had suggested adding a few more young people to their party, but Lydia had declined. Frances's mother insisted that she stay close to their wagon that evening, and Lydia couldn't bear to hear the other girls chatter on about how dreamy Private Gleason or Private Wilson or, worst of all, Corporal Brown was. Surely she and Nathan would be safe with Harpy along.

She sobbed, and the warrior tightened his grasp on her. He was not gentle, and the stench of his unwashed body and buckskin leggings was nauseating. Mentally Lydia christened him "Skunk."

To her left, Nathan yelped, and she saw that he was slipping down the side of the pinto mustang his captor rode. His horse had no saddle, and she was amazed the boy hadn't rolled off sooner.

"Nathan!" she cried, and Skunk squeezed her roughly. Their horse moved ahead of the other as Nathan tumbled to the ground, and she tried to look around and see what happened to him, but her kidnapper went on relentlessly, ignoring his companion's trouble.

Run, Nathan, she thought, but no, he could never outrun the horse, and they were too far from the wagon train now for him to make it back on his own. Little cover was available for him to hide in, although they seemed to be approaching a line of jagged hills.

Several minutes passed before she heard steady hoofbeats, coming fast from behind. She turned her head and caught a glimpse of Nathan, small and meek in front of the garishly painted warrior who brought him. She hoped he hadn't been injured or punished for falling off the mustang. Skunk jerked her arm sharply. She gasped and turned forward, concentrating on not sliding up too far on the horse's neck.

The warrior on the horse in front stopped, and they all came to a halt and clustered around him, the horses breathing deeply. The man who led them grunted, and the others stilled themselves and their mounts, listening. Lydia was suddenly afraid but at the same time hopeful. For the last hour she had prayed silently to God for a rescue but had doubted it would come soon. Dorcas probably hadn't started worrying until after full dark.

I don't ask for an earthquake or a legion of angels, Lord, she prayed. *Just let us live.*

Then she heard it—faint and rhythmic, the hoofbeats coming over the dry prairie behind them. Quick words were exchanged among the Sioux. While they were occupied, she stared at Nathan, trying to communicate silently to him her growing anticipation. She could make out his wide, frightened eyes and pale face. She wished she could speak to him, but she was afraid to. If she spoke, she would draw the wrathful attention of their abductors.

The leader wheeled his horse and headed off again, and the others followed. They went faster this time. The rugged mustang lunged into a rough canter, lowering his head, and Lydia was terrified. If the horse stumbled, she would fly forward headfirst. She laced her fingers tightly in his coarse mane. The warrior's arm was like a bar of iron around her waist, holding her firmly against him, and she could feel his breath on the back of her neck. Hard objects that formed his large necklace pressed into her back, and she wriggled. It only made the poking worse, and she wondered if the thing digging into her shoulder blade was a bear claw. *God, help us,* she pleaded.

They tore on over increasingly broken ground, dodging rocks and hollows. They came to the shadow of the hills and began climbing, and she felt a bit more secure as the horse met the incline, head still lowered.

She could hear the pursuers clearly now. The Sioux obviously did not relish an encounter with them. There was always the off chance they were Indians, too, perhaps from a rival tribe, but Lydia would not think of that. Surely God had answered her prayers, and the soldiers from the wagon train were in pursuit.

The warrior with Nathan came alongside them, and she saw the boy sliding once more toward the off side, clutching wildly at the pony's mane and the woven hair reins.

Skunk allowed his mustang to slow to a punishing trot, and she felt herself tossed about as badly as Nathan. The Indian transporting him was less skillful than Skunk at keeping an active hostage subdued. It seemed inevitable that Nathan would fall again. He was almost close enough for her to reach over and touch him if she had dared to let go her hold, and his mouth and eyes were wide in horror.

"Nathan! Jump!" she cried, confident that the pursuers were now close behind them. Skunk shoved his arm into her stomach so violently she felt faint. She gulped air and watched as Nathan began to struggle against his captor. The horse gave a squeal and hopped to the side, and Nathan catapulted to the ground.

వ

They were close, very close. Mike knew they would have only a brief moment of opportunity. As soon as the Sioux realized only two men pursued them, they would probably turn on them. It was darker now, and scrub brush grew more thickly in the hills. The ground was rockier, and he knew their quarry could hear the hoofbeats of their shod horses. If the Indians stopped to listen well, they would know how few pursued them. He had to keep them on the run as he closed the distance so they wouldn't stop and know what they were facing.

Lydia was the one he was most worried about. Nathan could survive for days or weeks if it took them that long to retrieve him. He was young enough to see it later as a grand adventure, to brag about it to his friends by the fireside.

But Lydia. That was another story.

The Sioux were supposed to be friendly now. There had been some trouble last summer, but the situation had cooled off, and there hadn't been any Indian incidents along the escort's section of the trail other than horse stealing and pilfering. Some mules and trade goods had been stolen from a band of merchants on their way from Fort Laramie to Fort Bridger a month ago, but they were thankful to have gotten through uninjured and considered it a business loss. Still, that was why the Oregon Escort operated. There was no guarantee. The problem remained heated enough for the government to consider building another fort between Fort Laramie and

Independence Rock, a new outpost to provide added security for travelers.

The riders in front of them were climbing a rocky hillside. Although they didn't seem to be following a trail, the Sioux knew where they were going. Maybe they had reinforcements up ahead. Mike decided to press them hard, to force a confrontation as soon as possible.

Paine's roan came along beside him, breathing heavily. Mike was surprised Beauty hadn't fallen back yet, exhausted and heaving, after their long day of hunting. Life on the trail had toughened the horse. Still, he regretted not taking a few minutes to ride back and tell Reese about the kidnapping and choose a fresh mount. If he'd known how far ahead the Sioux were, he'd have counted the time well spent. He'd been foolish and listened to Paine, the distraught father. The lives of the captives might depend on their strength, and the odds were against him and Paine.

He spurred Sam, exulting as the gelding edged up little by little, chasing the white rump of a mustang that trailed the other ponies.

There was a sudden shuffle up ahead, and the last mustang shied and leaped over something. Mike realized that one of the Indians' horses had stopped, and he was swiftly riding up on a mounted Sioux warrior.

He reined Sam in and raised his rifle, squinting to determine whether the Indian had either Lydia or Nathan with him. Then he realized that the shadow on the ground was moving. One of them had fallen, and the warrior had stopped to retrieve the captive.

Before Mike's brain told his finger to pull the trigger, Paine's rifle cracked close beside him, and Sam squealed and hopped away from Beauty. The Sioux sat still for an instant, staring at them. The ringing in Mike's ears receded.

"Couldn't have missed him clean," Paine said in disgust.

Mike hesitated no longer, but even as he fired, the warrior sagged and toppled from his mustang, and he knew Paine's shot had been true.

The others were far ahead, not stopping to make a stand with their companion. Mike urged Sam forward and stopped beside a dark heap on the ground.

"It's Nathan!"

Paine was already dismounting, and Mike jumped down beside him.

"Nathan, it's your papa!" Paine cradled the boy in his arms.

Mike's heart was racing. The boy could have broken his neck in the fall. He squatted beside his friend and said gently, "Let me check his pulse."

The boy moaned, and Paine laughed in relief. "Thank You, Lord!"

Nathan opened his eyes. "Papa?"

"Yes, yes, son. Are you all right?"

"My leg hurts something fierce."

Mike quickly reached to feel the boy's legs, tenderly running his hand from Nathan's right ankle up to his knee and beyond. When he touched the left ankle, Nathan gasped and shuddered.

"You'll be all right," his father assured him.

"Harpy?" Nathan gasped.

"He's dead, son."

"I thought so. That Injun that's got Miss Lydia hurt him when he starting barking at them. Papa, I was scared."

"We've got to get Miss Jackson," Paine said.

Mike looked toward the dark hills. "The boy's hurt. We can't go chasing after them with Nathan, but we can't leave him here alone."

"We'll lose those savages in this terrain. We've got to get her back, Mike."

"I know." His mind whirled, but he could see only one way. "If I wait for Reese's detachment, we could lose her forever. Or we might not find her again until—well, we need to find her soon. Now that they've lost the boy and one of their clan, they'll be angry. They might take it out on her."

Paine nodded somberly. "I'll head back with Nathan. No

other choice. You take care, Mike."

"I think Nathan's leg is broken. You should wait here for the others and make a travois to haul him back on."

Paine shook his head. "Can't, Mike. You need help. What if Reese decided to wait until daylight? We can't take that chance." He looked down anxiously at his son. "You're tough, boy. Can you make it back with me on Beauty?"

"I'll try, Papa."

"We'll go," Paine said to Mike, "even if I have to lead the horse and walk every step, but we'll keep moving."

"That mustang's foraging yonder," Mike said, nodding toward where he could discern the bulk of the Sioux pony. "Maybe you can get him for Nathan. Can you splint his leg?"

"No wood around here." Paine stood up. "Don't worry about us, Mike. And don't give up on us. We'll be back in force. If those Sioux reach a village, you'd better just sit back and wait for help."

"We'll see. I just know I've got to stick with them now, and I may have already waited too long. God be with you, Josiah."

Mike swept Sam's reins up and leaped into the saddle, heading off to where the four warriors had disappeared with Lydia. He wanted to reload his rifle, but it was dark, and every second counted. He decided to wait until he could hear the horses up ahead of him again, until he knew where they were. If need be, he would rely on his pistol and knife.

❧

Lydia writhed and wriggled, but Skunk was not about to let her escape. The other three warriors surged ahead of them on their horses, easily outrunning them with their lighter loads. She'd heard shots fired, and she tried to twist around and see if Nathan's captor was following them, but Skunk punched her in the side, knocking the air out of her. She sat as still as she could, sucking in ragged breaths, her knees gripping the horse's withers and her hands tangled in his mane.

The horse slowed, laboring up the rocky slope. Lydia strained for sounds of pursuit but heard nothing save the hoofbeats and the heaving and snorting of the Indians' mounts.

"God, keep Nathan safe," she breathed. Things were changing too quickly for her to form a coherent prayer. Either Nathan had been recaptured, or she was alone in the nightmare now.

The horses' hooves struck stone with each step. The troopers wouldn't be able to track them. Lydia considered her options and hung on.

They rounded the side of the hill and wound along a ledge until she could see a great distance in the moonlight and realized they were high above the plain. Was there a Sioux village up here? Or were they counting on eluding the troopers in the craggy hills?

A long time had passed since they had left Nathan and his captor behind, and Lydia began to lose heart. Skunk was last in line, and she had heard nothing from behind them for some time. If Sergeant Reese and the men of the escort had been coming, they must have lost the trail of the Sioux party.

Suddenly Skunk reined in the mustang, and Lydia listened as the warrior did. He sat still and stiff, inclining his head toward the back trail. There! Surely she had heard metal on stone.

Skunk urged the mustang forward toward the others, and she saw the three horses ahead jostle each other, heading swiftly toward a declivity in the rocks. The leader halted and turned to face them. He had chosen the ground for a standoff. Lydia took a deep breath. Skunk's horse was still twenty yards behind the others. *It's now or never,* she thought.

She strained forward against his grip, then jerked back, smashing his nose with her skull. His grip loosened, and she jammed both elbows back hard into the warrior's ribs, kicked hard with the solid wooden heels of her shoes, and dove forward over the left side of the mustang's neck.

thirteen

They struggled for a moment, Skunk grappling and Lydia squirming and kicking on the trotting horse. She fell with a *thud*, landing hard on her shoulder and hip. Ignoring the pain, she rolled away from the mustang, down the incline. She slammed against a boulder and lay stunned for an instant, then scrambled into its shadow.

Hoofbeats sounded quite close to her, but she didn't dare raise her head. Crouching behind the rock, she renewed her fractured prayers.

Several shots were fired in rapid succession, and she cowered lower, hoping she was invisible in the darkness behind the rock. She had seen a rifle in a scabbard on the leader's pony when they were captured, but she was certain that Skunk's only weapons were arrows and a gruesome knife.

The squeal of an injured horse tore the silence, and Lydia waited, breathless. She heard a thrashing and thumping, then dead quiet. She fought the impulse to sit up and look, and instead squeezed lower, tinier.

"Easy, Sam, easy."

Her chin jerked up before she considered her peril, and Lydia stared with uncontainable joy into the darkness. There were more thrashing sounds and loud panting and groaning. She was certain the horse was in dire straits, and she was also certain it was Mike Brown's calm voice she had heard.

"Michael?" she called cautiously.

There was an instant's silence; then his voice came, soft and incredulous. "Lydia?"

"Over here." She moved to the side of the rock.

"Keep down," he hissed, and she flattened herself.

After a long moment she rose a few inches on her elbows

and peered toward the voice. She could see the dark mass that was the gelding. He didn't seem to be moving now. Brown was crouched beside him, working with frenzy at the saddle and gear.

Lydia inched toward him on all fours, her weighted skirt hindering her. She tugged it impatiently from beneath her knees and scrambled toward him.

"Have you got Nathan?" she breathed.

"His father took him and headed back to camp for reinforcements. Nathan broke his leg when he fell, or Paine would have stuck with me."

"You mean, there were just the two of you?"

"Unfortunately, yes."

Lydia swallowed hard. "I was hoping for the entire escort."

"Yes, well, I should have brought them. I'll regret that decision for the rest of my life."

"Under the circumstances, I'll settle for you."

He laughed shortly. "You may change your mind if those savages attack us now."

"Where are they?" She stared into the gloom.

He nodded toward the heights. "Yonder. Are you hurt?"

"Not badly. A few bruises."

"Thank God." He bent to his task again.

"What are you doing?" The blade of his knife gleamed as he sliced the leather strap that suspended the saddlebags from the cantle of the saddle.

"The other saddlebag is trapped under the horse, but this one has the cartridges and caps for my revolver." He pulled the leather bag free of the saddle and grabbed her arm. "Get down. I'm not sure how close they are."

"Is Sam dead?"

"As good as. Shot him right out from under me. I didn't know they had rifles."

"Only one, I think. The one who grabbed me didn't have a gun; I know that."

"How many are there?"

"There were five at first, but Nathan fell off his horse, and the one who was bringing him stopped."

"You don't have to worry about that one."

She caught her breath. "Good. Four, then."

"Come on, we'd better get away from Sam. They may be analyzing the situation. If they know I'm the only one out here with you, they'll move in for sure." He grasped her hand and pulled her down the slope toward a large cluster of rocks. Lydia sank to the ground and sat with her back to a boulder, rubbing her sore shoulder.

"All right," Mike said. "Let's get our breath."

"Then we head back to the wagon train?"

"No. We hide until daylight or until some help comes. But we'll have to find a better place to hole up. We don't stand a chance in the open on foot against those Sioux. Besides, my ankle took a beating when Sam went down."

"Is it broken?"

"I don't think so, or I wouldn't have been able to get this far. But we need a hideaway with a small opening, or a high spot with a good view of all approaches. Someplace where I can defend our position."

They sat without speaking for several minutes. In the faint light, Lydia watched him reload the empty chambers of his Colt Dragoon revolver.

"Do you have a rifle?" She almost hated to ask.

"It's back there. I'd fired it earlier, and the ammunition was in the other saddlebag. You hungry?"

"I—well, yes."

He thrust something into her hand. "Eat."

"Jerky?"

"Yes. Josiah and I took some with us hunting."

"Who?"

"Mr. Paine."

"It's Josiah? Really?"

"Really." He carefully stowed his equipment back in the leather pouch. "I've got my pistol, Lydia. That and my knife.

Our best defense is to stay hidden. You understand?"

"Yes."

"All right. I'd like to get farther from the horse, to a more secure spot, but in this darkness we might stumble around and make enough noise to draw their attention. If they're scouting for us, we might even run into them."

"You're sure they'll come back?"

"Pretty sure. The Sioux like to recover their dead. They may have circled back to pick up their friend's body, but then they'll want revenge."

"How will we know if our friends come?"

"Don't worry. You'll know when the cavalry arrives."

They sat silent for a long time. Lydia was very tired and sore, but her nerves kept her wide awake. Over and over, her mind reviewed the scene by the river when she and Nathan had gloated over the plump, fragrant blackberries.

Suddenly, Harpy had stiffened and growled at a thicket.

"Come here, Harpy!" Nathan had called, but the dog had taken a step toward the thicket, still growling. Lydia felt fear then. A bear could be behind those bushes. They were entering the mountains, and she'd heard enormous bears lived out there.

Harpy barked and leaped toward the bushes. He was in midair when the brambles parted and a copper-skinned man met his lunge. Before Lydia could register what was happening, the dog lay bleeding on the turf, and strong hands seized her from behind.

"Nathan could have got away," she whispered to Mike. "They caught me first, and he grabbed a stick and ran at Skunk."

"Skunk?"

She smothered a laugh. "That's what I called the one who caught me. Oh, not to his face, of course."

"Of course. You're too well-bred for that."

"Well, if you could have smelled him—"

"I'm gratified that wasn't necessary."

A giggle burbled up in her throat. "Stop it. You're making me laugh."

"Laughter does good like a medicine."

"Not when your life depends on silence," she said ruefully.

"That's true. But I'm glad you can see the humor of it." His warm hand found hers, and he squeezed her fingers. Lydia's heart began to pound. "So Nathan tried to defend you," he said.

"Yes. He should have run away."

"They would have caught him, maybe killed him."

She thought about that. "I'm glad you're here, Michael."

He sighed. "Can't help it, I guess. I'm glad, too. I mean, since you're here. If you weren't, well, there's lots of places I'd rather be." He shifted and stretched his left leg out gingerly.

"Should you take your boot off?" Lydia asked.

"I don't think that would be wise right now."

❧

Mike thought once that he heard faint hoofbeats, but he wasn't certain. Lydia was drowsing, slumped against the rock, breathing softly. His ankle throbbed, and now and then a stab of pain shot through it. He watched the quarter moon move slowly across the sky. It would set soon. He gritted his teeth and moved forward to where he could see a larger area of the night-shrouded hill, surveying the terrain while he still had the moon's light.

He picked out a likely spot they could move to, a tumble of large rocks at the bottom of a cliff west of the path the Sioux had taken. He judged the distance and wiggled his toes. His painful ankle might give out on him if he tried to run on it. But with Lydia's help, he could make it to the sanctuary below the cliff. He frowned, eyeing that cliff. It would be much better if they could gain the top, but he doubted his injury would allow that.

The stealthiest *swish* reached his ears, and he froze against the rock. He looked all around, slowly, deliberately, his revolver poised, trying to shelter behind the rock as much as possible. He couldn't see anything unusual, and he sat still, waiting and listening. He had just begun to relax when he glimpsed an unnatural movement between a large rock and a bush. Something had made a move, using the terrain for cover, and it was coming closer.

"Michael?"

He'd thought she was sound asleep.

"Stay back," he whispered, not taking his eyes from the brush.

"What is it?"

"They're getting ready."

She was quiet, but he could feel her nervous energy. She was dying to ask more questions, to wriggle her way up beside him and look out over the landscape. But she stayed put.

Lord, I've been a foolish man this day, and now I've wound up in a bad spot. Out here in the middle of nowhere with a helpless woman, and I've got four savages trying to kill me. That wouldn't be so bad, if it weren't for her. If they get through me, she's a goner, Lord, and I just can't let that happen. You can't. Please.

The prayer was only in his mind, but he had no doubt that it was heard. He thought of David hiding out in the hills of Palestine and his pleas to God. *"Lo, the wicked bend their bow, they make ready their arrow upon the string, that they may privily shoot at the upright in heart."* He sat waiting, watching, listening, and struggling to put together the fragments of information his senses brought him.

He heard another tiny sound. They were out there, all right. The moon was setting, and they would soon have nothing but starlight. He had hoped they would wait until dawn, but these were crafty enemies. They probably knew he was alone by now. They'd found Sam, and the single set of shod hoofprints wherever there was dirt would tell the story. They knew he was at a disadvantage. They would also realize that if they waited, a larger force would come after the girl.

A dark wraith tore from the bush to a hollow in the ground, and he almost fired the pistol but steadied himself. *Wait until you can't miss,* he counseled himself.

He heard Lydia stir behind him. *Don't talk now,* he pleaded inwardly. He hugged the rock, hoping the moonlight wasn't glinting off his gun barrel.

A rush of movement came from behind him, and Lydia screamed. He turned and found a warrior had jumped to the top of the rock she was leaning on, knife ready to strike.

Mike fired, then whipped around. As he had feared, another Sioux was only yards away, with his bow drawn. Mike fired his pistol again and dove behind the rock. An arrow zipped past him and plunked when it struck behind him.

Lydia!

He peeked out, but the archer was no more to be seen. With dread, he turned and took a deep breath. Lydia was lying prone, staring at him with wide, luminous eyes.

"Where's the Sioux I shot?"

She looked toward the top of the rocks. "He fell backward over the rock. I think it was Skunk. I smelled him."

Mike exhaled shakily. "We need to move."

"They'll see us."

"The moon's almost down. It will be darker. We can't stay here." He heard a faint scrabbling sound and reached quickly for Lydia's wrist. "Shh. He's out there."

"Behind the rock," she agreed, worming closer to him. "He's alive."

Mike looked out toward where the bowman had been. "Come here."

She crept up beside him and stared out at the night.

"I've got four shots left before I have to reload. You see those rocks over there?"

"Yes. It's too far, Mike."

"No. See, there's some jack pine between here and there, and some more rocks. We can make it. Head for that rock first, and I'll be right behind you."

"What if there's an Indian behind that rock?"

"They don't want to hurt you. And I won't let them take you again, Lydia."

She hesitated.

"On three." He put steel in his voice so she wouldn't argue. "One, two—"

She broke from the cover of the rock and bolted to the next refuge. Mike followed, darting glances toward the most likely hiding places for the Sioux. Lydia flung herself behind the rock, and he looked back at their old hiding place. A shadow grew tall by the rocks, and he fired his revolver in its direction, knowing it went wild, but it was enough to make the Indian take cover where they had been seconds ago.

"You all right?" Lydia said in his ear. Her hands grasped his shoulder and his arm. Something hard poked him in the side.

"I'm fine. What's this?"

"The arrow they shot at us back there. It stuck in the ground right beside me."

He blinked. A souvenir? At a time like this, she was picking up mementos? "Let's keep moving. That was way too close."

"That brush over there?"

"Yes, and keep going right through it until you hit those scrub trees. Wait for me there."

"You should reload."

"No time. Go."

fourteen

Ten minutes later, Lydia lay panting in a hollow between several large rocks. She'd feared they would be exposed from above once more, but Mike had found a place where she could ease back into a crevice with the rocks meeting over her. They were both gasping for breath while he fumbled with his cartridges in the dark.

"How's your ankle?" she asked, setting the arrow carefully beside her.

"Bad. I forgot about it while we were running, but I'm paying for that now."

"I wish I could do something."

"Is this where you rip up your petticoats to make me a bandage?"

She laughed. "Wouldn't you just love that?"

"No. It would be a waste of good cloth and expensive lace."

"That's all you know. This one has a simple tatted edging."

"Made it yourself?"

"Of course. It was part of our training. It took three yards to trim the flounce."

"Well, I'm glad I didn't get shot. You'd have to take all that lace off before I'd let you rip your linen into bandages. There." He sat back, and she knew he was finished reloading.

"How can you do that in the dark? I can't see a thing."

"There's a little light here. Not much. Take this."

"What?" She reached toward him, and her hand bumped something hard. She felt it and realized it was his bone-handled knife.

"But I—"

"Take it." He wasn't looking at her but instead out between the rocks toward the small pines.

Lydia grasped the hilt of the knife.

"Squeeze back between the rocks. Make yourself small."

"Michael—"

"Now, Lydia. Please."

She obeyed, sitting down in the snug niche and pulling her knees up before her. She tucked her skirt around her. When she sat back, she could barely see Mike's silhouette against the opening. The silence was frightening. He sat motionless, and if she hadn't known of his injury, she'd have thought him ready to spring, catlike, at whatever showed itself at the edge of the rocks.

"Michael," she whispered.

She thought his mouth curved upward for an instant as he turned his profile to her in the starlight. "What is it?"

"I think I misjudged you."

"Oh, you changed your mind, and you think I'm a gentleman now?" He was definitely smiling.

"I wouldn't go that far, but I was wrong about you."

"You thought I was an indolent churl."

"I never said indolent. You're a hardworking man."

"Oh, excuse me, I meant insolent."

She couldn't help chuckling but sobered as she noted his wary posture and the way his keen glance roved over the area and avoided resting on her.

"I wanted to say. . .well, if things go badly—"

He waited a moment. "Well, if what?"

"Thank you."

"Forget it. Just concentrate on living."

"Yes, but—"

She broke off as he raised his left hand suddenly. It hung motionless for an instant; then he brought it together with his right, on the butt of the pistol, steadying it.

Lydia held her breath and stared out between the rocks where Brown stared. What did he see?

They came in a rush, all four of the warriors, and Mike fired rapidly. Lydia pressed her hands over her ears, but the noise was painful in the tiny cavern. Each shock reverberated, numbing her.

He used four shots in quick succession, but even so, one warrior made it to the entrance of their haven. Terror welled up in her as she watched him come closer and closer. Mike's gun must be empty. She clutched the knife.

At the last possible second, Mike pulled the trigger, and the Sioux fell within a yard of the gap in the rocks. She listened, but her ears still rang.

"Are they gone?" She could barely hear her own words.

Mike shook his head.

She rubbed her ears. After a long moment, the ringing lessened. She touched the back of his gray cotton shirt, and Mike reached back and found her hand while still watching the opening.

"How are we doing?" she asked.

"This nearest one's dead for sure. I think I hit one of the others, but he didn't fall."

"Get me the bow."

He turned and stared at her then. "What?"

"The bow! You can reach it."

"Are you crazy?"

"I told you I learned archery."

"Oh, right, Miss Cluckson's."

"Clarkson's."

"You can't mean to use that thing."

"I won the medal three years running."

"What did you shoot at?"

"Paper targets set up against a straw stack."

"Well, if I see any paper targets for you to shoot at, I'll let you know."

"Let me get it," she insisted, trying to shove past him.

He pushed her back, a bit roughly, Lydia thought.

"You stay put," he hissed. He looked out again, cautiously, then took his hat off and held it outside the shelter of the rocks. All was quiet. He bent swiftly forward and grabbed the fallen warrior's bow. As he ducked back inside the hideaway, a gunshot cracked, and chips splintered from the stone by his head.

"Get back!" He pushed her to the rear of the cavern again, tossing the bow after her, and sat motionless and wary, listening.

After half a minute had passed, he said softly, "I'm sorry. Are you all right?"

"Yes, but. . ."

"But what?"

"You didn't get me any extra arrows."

⁊

Lydia was quiet for a long time, and Mike's admiration for her grew. He heard her fingering the bow. Well, let her. It gave her something to think about. Still, he shouldn't have risked his neck for it.

"Think they're gone?" she whispered at last.

"No. They'll make one more attack."

"How do you know?"

"They went for me and got my horse. That wasn't according to plan, I'm sure. They'd have liked to keep Sam. They always want more horses. Then they attacked us at our first hideout and followed us here for another go-round. One more time before they decide whether or not to call if off. Four times."

"Four times? Is that lucky for them or something?"

"It's a sacred number. They're funny. Sometimes they quit when the first man falls. But if they decide they want revenge, then look out!"

"There's three of them left, you think?"

"Maybe. Did you get a look at this one? Is it Skunk?"

Lydia sidled up to him, and he felt the warmth radiating from her and realized he was cold. He'd left his wool uniform jacket in camp that morning when he and Paine set out for a day of hunting in the late July sun.

"I can't tell," she whispered.

The warrior was lying face down. "You said he had a knife.

What about his clothes? His hair?"

"No," she said quickly. "Skunk had a big necklace with lots of beads and things hanging from it. Bones, too." She grimaced, and he imagined she'd been all too close to the Indian's jewelry.

"Well, I'm pretty sure Old Skunk is hurting, and one of his buddies, too. Maybe they'll call it quits."

"You don't believe that, though."

Mike looked up at the stars. "It's still a long time 'til dawn."

"How can you tell?"

"By the phase of the moon. It's down now, but it'll be awhile before you see the sun."

"Huh. It seems like we've been out here for hours."

"Not so very long. Did Miss Parkman teach you any astronomy?"

"Clarkson."

"Right."

"No, she didn't."

He shifted and reached for her hand. "Well, now, that school needs some improvement in its curriculum. Bend over here. Can you see those stars that form sort of a square? Over the trees there."

She peered upward in the direction he indicated. "I'm not sure."

"See the tallest pine? Let your eyes travel straight up from it. There are four stars in a box and three that form the handle of the dipper."

"You mean that's the Big Dipper?"

"Yes."

"My father used to try to show it to me, and I could never see it."

"But you see it now?"

"I think so."

"Well, then, let's see if you can see the Little Dipper. Look at the two stars that make the front edge of the Big Dipper. They're the pointers. Follow a straight line up from them until you see a bright star."

"Way up there?"

"Yes. That's the North Star. It's the tail end of the Little Dipper."

"You're joking."

"No, I'm not. The little one's tipped opposite the big one, like it's pouring syrup into it. That's what my daddy taught me."

"I see it! And to think, I had to almost lose my scalp to learn to find the North Star." Lydia sighed and crumpled into a little heap.

"What's the matter, darlin'?" He pulled out his most Southern drawl to distract her, but for once she didn't scold him for his flippancy.

"It seems like years since Nathan and I went to pick blackberries."

"Sleep if you can."

"No. If they're coming back, I need to be alert. You'd better reload."

"If I start, that's when they'll come."

"They can't know. I'll watch while you do it."

"All right. I'm down to one shot, and I guess that wouldn't do us much good. But don't stick your head out there." He worked quickly, but even so, it took him a couple of minutes to fish the components from the saddlebag and reload the pistol in the gloom. When he was done, he looked at Lydia. She was sitting back from the opening but was watching intently, scanning the rough hillside. The bow she held across her lap looked almost like a toy. Her mouth was set in a grim line as she searched for the smallest movement.

Lord, keep her safe. I surely can't do this on my own. I'll take whatever You hand me, but we can't hold out forever, and this gal. . . He remembered her woeful demeanor during their conversation the night he'd gone with her to fetch Dorcas's skillet. *Lord, give her peace.*

He slid toward her, feeling a renewed resolution. "All set."

She didn't move back. "Michael, I could get his quiver."

He smiled. She was scrappy, all right.

"Better not chance it, darlin'."

She looked at him sharply, then crawled back into the depths of the crevice.

≈

Lydia ran her hands over the strung bow again. It was much shorter than the ones they had used in Hartford. The springy wood was smooth on the belly of the bow, but it was backed with something hard as a fingernail that seemed to be elastic. Maybe animal sinew. The string was a tough, twisted cord. She tested the pull. It was much harder than what she was used to, but she thought she could draw it back far enough to make her arrow deadly. There was barely room in the tiny cave, but if an enemy filled the doorway, she could hardly miss.

She picked up her one arrow. The point was bound into a slit on the end of the slender shaft. It felt like metal, but it might be stone. She thought of the blunt brass tips they had used at Miss Clarkson's and gritted her teeth. Mike was right about one thing—this wasn't target practice. Those were real, living men out there. Could she use the lethal force of the short bow against them?

It took only the memory of Harpy to tell her she could. How swiftly and unfeelingly they had killed the dog. They would have killed Mike, too, with as little concern.

Mike tensed, and she sat up straighter. "Stay back there. Get over to the side so you're not in the line of fire."

She obeyed him but slipped the nock of her arrow onto the string and held the bow at rest in front of her. She was more comfortable with it in her hands than with his razor-sharp knife. She slipped that into her high shoe top, just in case.

A rifle shot sounded, and Mike ducked back behind the rock. "Just stay under cover and let him use up his ammunition."

Her heart raced, and she was trembling. She hated that. If she had to fight tonight, she wanted her hands to be steady.

fifteen

Mike edged toward the gap to look out again, then moved rapidly to fire his pistol. Lydia covered her ears, slipping one hand through the bowstring and clinging to the arrow so she wouldn't lose it. The opening in the rocks was gray before her, and Mike crouched low, almost lying down.

She lowered her hands, but all she could hear was that awful ringing. Gradually she became aware of her own loud breathing.

"Michael!"

He didn't answer, at least not that she could hear, but he sat a little taller, looking outside.

She waited, trying to calm her breath, and without warning a volley of several arrows hit the rocks near her and shattered.

"Get down!" Mike shouted.

੨ঽ

Another cascade of arrows whistled into the cavern, and Mike knew he had to stop them. He had pinpointed the location of the warrior with the rifle behind a gnarled clump of brush. He wasn't so sure about the other two. He'd hoped at least one was out of the action, but from the intense fire, there had to be three of them left.

Doggedly, he watched the spot from which the gunfire had come, praying for a clear shot. It was close enough, but he couldn't just blaze away at them. His supply of lead and powder cartridges was nearly gone, and he wasn't known as a sharpshooter. Every bullet had to count.

He saw movement to his left and turned, knowing it was too late if the aim was true. An arrow hit the rock near him, shattering into pieces, and he fired at the archer. Finally, he found his mark. The jolt of exultation was short-lived. As he swiveled to deal with his other foes, the rifleman rose behind the bushes, and Mike steeled himself to get off two good shots, no matter what. Something hit him just below his collarbone. He aimed the revolver again, but it was very heavy. Pain shot through his arm and shoulder and chest. Using both hands, he leveled it as the Sioux lowered his own weapon. Mike pulled the trigger once more.

It was satisfying to see the warrior fall like a stone, his rifle barrel catching the starlight. Mike sank back against the rock, breathing in deep gasps, trying to realize what had happened. His shoulder was on fire, and his arm was going numb. The pistol fell from his hand with a *thunk*.

I can't quit now, Lord. There's one more out there. If he saw me go down, he'll close in for the kill and take Lydia. Please don't let it end like this.

"Michael!" Lydia was pulling him away from the opening. "Mike! Get back!"

"My gun's empty, darlin'." His tongue didn't want to form the words, and she knelt close beside him, staring at him. He caught the glitter of fear in her eyes.

"Are you hit?"

"Afraid so."

"Michael! You can't—"

She tugged at his boots, pulling him clumsily to the side. He moaned at the pain that shot through his ankle and his shoulder. A tearing sound jerked him to full consciousness.

"What are you doing?" She didn't answer, but he knew. "Don't do that!"

"This is the time, Michael. No jokes now. You're bleeding."

"Three yards of lace. . ." He hated the way his voice trailed off. "Is it bad?"

"No."

"You're lying, aren't you?"

"Yes." He took a deep breath and focused on the stars above, then pushed himself up on his good elbow. "Lydia, forget about me. He thinks you're alone now. He thinks you're defenseless."

Lydia stopped her frantic preparations. "Aren't I?"

"Only if you think you are. I'm not dead yet, sweetheart, but I can't be much help to you. You've got several things going for you, though, the biggest one being God's power."

She exhaled slowly. "I've never felt very powerful, Mike."

"You don't have to. It's not a feeling. It's knowing that if God doesn't want that savage to haul you out of here, it won't happen."

"I've been praying," she said hesitantly.

"That's fine, but God's also given you some resources."

She caught a sharp breath. "You mean the bow?"

It sounded ludicrous, even to him, but he knew he couldn't fight the last Sioux off with only a knife in his present condition.

"He may be coming, even now. Get over there and watch."

Still she hesitated.

"Lydia! I don't want to have to tell Dan Reese I got them all but one, and then lost you again. I'd never live it down."

She scurried to the opening, and he leaned back with a sigh. It wasn't his reputation he was worried about, but that seemed to have jolted her into action. He closed his eyes. *Lord, it's up to You now. Don't let me lose her again. Please!*

☙

Lydia sat panting in the doorway, shivering and staring out into the night. Her faith had always been an important part of her life, but right now it seemed tiny and fragile. Would God really give her the strength to fight for her life? *Lord, I can't do this*, she cried silently. *Mike says You'll give me power, but I'm so frightened! I don't know if I can hold the bow steady!*

She fingered it tentatively.

"Don't let him get close to you," Mike's weary voice came from behind her. "Don't let him get within arm's length, because once he gets hold of you, it's all over. You understand?"

"Yes." She crouched between the rocks, sending up broken prayers. Had the Sioux given up? Was their fourth attack ended? And would she sit here all keyed up until dawn wondering, while Mike's life drained from him?

She thought she heard a sound. Maybe it was a breeze in

the stunted pines. There had been no wind all night, though. She eased the bow into position and nocked the arrow.

Lord, help me now. If Michael dies, I'm not sure I want to live, either.

She thought of just standing up in the open, inviting the warrior to put an end to this miserable contest.

"Sweetheart, be careful."

She turned toward his voice.

"Don't look at me. Look for him."

Quickly she faced the opening again. "There's only one?"

"I'm pretty sure. If he's shooting, get down. If he's running toward you, wait until he's three strides away."

She willed her heart to ease its thumping. "I don't know if I can do it, Mike."

He laughed, and she caught her breath.

"You? You took the medal three years running."

Yes, she thought. *Yes, I did. Lord, Your will be done.*

He stirred behind her, and she asked shakily, "Are you going to make it, Mike? Tell me the truth."

"Well, it didn't hit my lung. Where's my knife?"

"In my shoe."

"Left or right?"

"Right."

"Come closer."

She inched back toward him, watching the doorway, and felt his hand grasp her ankle.

"Sorry, darlin'. I'm not much use right now, but I'll be your last line of defense. Just remember, that man doesn't want you dead. He's determined to ride into his village with all his friends' horses and a captive."

"You guarantee that?"

"Nothing's guaranteed with the Lakota. He could be gone now, slinking off toward home, but I don't think so."

She faced the opening again with determination, keeping well to the side behind the rock. Another arrow whizzed into their refuge.

"Easy," Mike said. "If that didn't split, you've got another arrow. And if we keep over to this side, he can't hit us from out there. Just be careful about showing yourself. If he thinks you're me, he won't hesitate to fire."

Lord, only You can help us now, she prayed. *Help me not to be foolish and waste all of Michael's effort. I want us both to live. If we can't be together after today, so be it. Just please, don't let this fine man die in vain.*

Cautiously she leaned to her right, almost expecting a hail of bullets in response. All was quiet. She held her breath and peered out into the night. Suddenly she saw him, crouching, as still as she was, in the shadow of a boulder scarcely ten yards away. He was looking at her. She recognized his cruel sneer, and fear surged up inside her. She wanted to duck back into the dark, to get away from his piercing stare, but she sensed that if she wavered now, he would come and drag her from the hiding place.

She moved forward into the gap between the rocks, and he rose on his knees, raising his bow. Lydia held her arrow on the string, knowing that once she drew it back she would not be able to hold it long.

"Skunk!" He might not understand her derisive name for him, but he would recognize her voice. She saw the surprise register on his painted face. The dawn was coming, and with it light enough to let her see her enemy's lips twitch.

He stood and began walking toward her.

"Stop!" she called.

Skunk came on slowly with the placid smile of a cat.

She gulped a breath and raised her bow, drawing back the string with the same motion. He stopped a few paces away, eyeing her with speculation, then said something in his own language. Lydia didn't move an eyelash. He stooped and laid his bow down.

He spoke again, almost gently, extending his hand toward her. Lydia didn't know if she could hold the string back much longer. She clenched her teeth.

Skunk snarled and pulled his knife from its sheath and took a step toward her.

She let the arrow fly and watched in mixed relief and horror as it found its mark. Skunk opened his mouth in utter surprise, and she watched him fall. It was like the game Statues she and the other girls had played at Miss Clarkson's, whirling around with hands clasped, then letting go and freezing in whatever odd posture they found themselves. Skunk sank to the ground, still holding the knife out menacingly.

sixteen

Mike battled the sharp pain and inched toward the opening in the rocks where Lydia stood. She had shot her arrow, and now she was exposed to any enemies left outside their haven.

"Get back!" He pulled himself up beside her, leaning against the largest rock. She turned to look at him, tears streaming down her cheeks.

"I—I did it."

He looked past her and squinted, a strange, expectant awe overpowering his pain and hopelessness. The last of the warriors lay still on the hillside, just five yards from their shelter. Mike swallowed hard.

"Well! I can't wait to see your fancy stitchery."

Lydia sobbed, and he immediately regretted his callousness. She was trembling, and he reached to pull her to him.

"Darlin', I'm sorry. Let's take a second to thank God here."

She collapsed against him, weeping uncontrollably, and Mike gasped as the pain shot through him. He despised his weakness and set his back more firmly against the rock, determined not to fall over.

"Lord, we thank You for life," he said, holding her perhaps more tightly than was proper, but it was necessary if he wanted to stay upright. "We thank You for victory. Now let us rejoin our friends if that's part of Your will, Lord."

"Thank you," Lydia whispered raggedly, and he squeezed her. She had stopped crying, and if his shoulder hadn't hurt so badly, he'd have tremendously enjoyed holding her in his arms.

"Sweetheart, if I don't sit down right now, I'll probably fall down."

She jumped back. "Oh, Mike, I'm sorry."

He settled on the ground, keeping his back to the rock,

grimacing as he extended his injured ankle.

"Your shirt is all blood! You've got to let me do something." She turned away, and he knew she was about to sacrifice her petticoats for sure, in spite of his earlier pleas.

"I knew you could do it," he said, hoping he could make her smile again.

"You did not. You thought I was bluffing."

"No, but maybe I did think you were a little optimistic."

She laughed without mirth. "He had almost the same stubborn look you get sometimes." She paused with the finely woven white cloth in her hands. "He was so human then. I didn't know if I could—oh, Mike, it was awful."

"I'm sure it was."

"He changed all of a sudden, and I knew that if I didn't go with him, he would kill me." Her eyes were huge. She scrambled to look out between the rocks, then came slowly back to his side, the white petticoat trailing from her hand.

"He–he's still lying there." Her lower lip quivered.

Mike sent up a quick, silent prayer.

"Do you know that verse in Psalm 18 that says, 'He teacheth my hands to war'?"

She shook her head, her eyes glistening. "I loved archery. I never thought. . ."

Mike said quickly, "But God knew. He prepared you for this moment. I'm sorry I made fun of your education before. It did seem a bit frivolous at the time, but I was forgetting that with God, nothing is wasted."

She nodded. "Perhaps you're right. Now let me at that wound."

Mike tried to unbutton his shirt, but his right hand wouldn't function that well. He sighed and let her take over. "I've come to a momentous decision, Lydia."

"And what is that?" She bit her lip as she worked the buttons free from the stiffening fabric.

"I'm going to send all my children to Miss Clarkson's. Well, all my daughters, that is."

She looked into his eyes, startled, then laughed. "Hush, you. You're not trying to distract me while you breathe your last, are you?"

"Hardly. I'm tougher than that."

"Tough enough to ride a mustang back to the wagon train?"

"Oh, I don't know."

"There must be some ponies tethered near here," she said, working tenaciously at the buttons.

"Probably at their war lodge. I think we're close to it."

"What's a war lodge?"

"It's a hut they use when they're out raiding. Just a small, hidden place made out of logs or hides or whatever's handy."

"You've seen one?"

"No, a friend told me about it. Trooper Barkley's brother. He's a scout for the army, and he's spent a lot of time with the Indians."

"I could go and look for it."

"No."

She arched her brows. "Why not?"

"Lydia, you must realize what we've just come through. It may not be safe out there, even now. I'm not letting you out of my sight."

"So. . .we wait here for the soldiers? What if Mr. Paine never made it back to the wagons?"

"He did. I won't believe otherwise, so don't say it."

She nodded slowly. "All right. Then they should be here soon."

He avoided looking directly at her. He'd expected Sergeant Reese and his men hours ago. They must not have started out until Paine returned to camp. If he returned. He glanced sharply at Lydia. He'd just told her not to say it, but the thought was still nibbling at the edge of his hope.

As they talked, Lydia tore a long strip of white cotton from the bottom of her petticoat and ripped off the lace edging. She folded the cloth into a thick pad. "Here. You're losing a lot of blood. We need to stop it."

He sprawled against the rock and let her pull the front of his shirt back and press the wad of cotton against the torn flesh. He winced but sat still as she pushed firmly on it. His eyes closed. The pain was intense, but the pressure gave him some relief.

⁂

Lydia sat for half an hour, pressing the folded cloth against his wound. Mike appeared to be drowsing, and after awhile she was sure he slept. She was glad. It meant his pain was not sharp enough to keep him awake. She watched him as the sun rose and bathed the hillside in light.

Lord, please let him recover, and let us get back to the train.

He jerked awake suddenly and stared at her, then sighed and shifted his position.

"How you doing?" she asked softly.

"Could be better."

"Do you think you're gaining strength? Because if you're getting weaker, there's no sense in waiting. I'll go look for those ponies and ride for help."

"No." She frowned at him, and Mike shrugged, then winced at the pain. "I'm not letting you go alone."

"I can find those mounts, Michael."

He shook his head. "Still stubborn."

"Still rude."

He smiled, watching her with half-closed eyes.

"Are you in pain?" she asked.

"Yes."

"Please let me go. I can't stand the thought of you bleeding to death while we sit here."

"I'm not bleeding to death."

"Well, this cloth is saturated, and I need to change it. Can you hold it for a minute?"

He reached over and pushed on the front of his shirt, where it covered the blood-soaked bandage. Lydia took his knife and started a tear at the edge of her petticoat, then ripped off another row of fabric.

"I hope you have more underthings in Paine's wagon."

"Insolent man. A true gentleman would never mention the source of these bandages." She folded the strip carefully, then faced him. "Ready?"

He opened his eyes. "Do you have to?"

"Your wound is still bleeding, Michael. It's soaked the bandage and your shirt."

He looked down at her blood-stained hands and the fresh wad of fabric. "Lydia, there's a missionary in the territory, west of Fort Hall."

"A missionary?"

"Yes. A preacher. Won't you please consider becoming my wife?"

She stared at him for just a second and wondered if he was delirious. She ignored the question and leaned forward to remove the bloody dressing from his wound.

"That's assuming I don't bleed to death," he amended.

"I told you, I can't." She pulled the old bandage away in one quick motion, then applied the fresh one firmly.

Mike groaned.

"Sorry. I'm afraid it's still oozing blood." She kept her gaze on her hands. She didn't think she could bear to look into his eyes just then.

"Why not, Lydia? You know you like me."

"Rubbish. I can't stand you."

"Is that so?"

"Yes, and you're much too ardent for a dying man."

He laughed, then sobered, and she couldn't keep from looking at him. His soft expression almost melted her determination to keep him at arm's length.

"What is it, darlin'? This contract you mentioned. It's not. . . a marriage contract, is it?"

"Of course not. Do you think I would actually. . ." She stared at him. The idea that she would put up with his attempts at flirtation while promised to marry another man was appalling. "Really, Michael."

He relaxed visibly, sinking back with a sigh. "I hoped it wasn't that, but I couldn't be sure. For all I knew, you were married already or had signed away your future and were planning to wed some fur trapper."

Lydia laughed. "That's silly."

"Well, there's only one other logical explanation. Mr. Paine said you were going to teach school, so I guess that's it—a business contract."

"Yes. It's very simple, really. I signed a document stating that I will not get married while I am teaching."

He was very still, and she concentrated on the bandage, holding it steadily with both hands and avoiding his gaze. He was just too magnetic. She wasn't sure if it was his personality or his tattered uniform or the possibility that his proposal was not part of the banter.

"They can do that?" he asked at last.

"They can. They have."

He reached up and stroked a loose lock of her hair back where it hung over her cheek. "Someone must have told them how beautiful you are, and they put that clause in the paper to make sure you didn't abandon your purpose when the men started buzzing around you."

She couldn't look at him. His fingers rested lightly on her cheek, just in front of her ear, and she was afraid that if she moved the slightest bit and met his eyes, he would pull her into his arms. But that was silly. He was badly wounded. How could a man in great pain think about courting, especially when the lady had told him she wasn't available?

He raised his chin suddenly and stared at her. "Is that the only reason you told me you couldn't be more than friends?"

"Yes."

"There's nothing else in the way?"

"Isn't that enough?"

She glanced toward him and realized immediately that it was a mistake. His fingers slid back into her hair, and he pulled her closer to him. "Lydia, I love you." His lips were inches from hers.

"You're serious." It came out as a whisper, as she realized he was about to kiss her.

"Dead serious."

She didn't draw back but closed her eyes and lost herself in that moment of delight, all the while trying to remember what it was she was supposed to be doing. She wanted to ease her hands up around his neck and return his embrace, but suddenly she remembered.

"Your wound," she gasped, pushing away from him, trying not to jostle his injured shoulder.

"Can you stand me now?"

"If I can, I shouldn't." Her pulse was thundering from the effect of his sweet kiss.

"What town are you going to be teaching in?"

"Never mind."

"Why?"

She shook her head. "I know you, and I don't want any knights in shining armor stirring up trouble for me with my employers."

"What, you think I'd challenge the school board to a duel?"

"I need this position, Mike." She looked into his eyes and nodded. "I do. And without even meaning to, you could get me fired. Just by making your presence known, you could cause trouble for me."

He was silent for a moment, then said, "If the security of a place to live is what you need. . .or an income. . ."

"Please stop."

"But Lydia, we're talking about the rest of our lives."

"Are we?" It was a timid squeak.

"I won't claim you love me, but you have to admit you at least like me."

She looked off toward the hillside and the plain beyond, breathing slowly and carefully. "Look, the troops may never come. Those Sioux ponies can't be far away."

"Quit changing the subject."

She scowled at him. "I don't want to talk about the school board."

"All right, fine. What do you want to talk about?"

"Why don't you tell me about your family?"

He said nothing for a moment, and Lydia felt her color rising. She didn't think she could stand it if he kept on talking about a future she knew was impossible.

"I really want to know about your family," she said.

"All right, come sit here beside me."

"I need to hold this."

"You can hold it from here."

"No."

"What? You doubt my motives?"

"Yes, actually."

"Oh, Lydia." He tugged gently on her arm, and she gave in, settling beside him on the ground. Somehow, she ended up in the curve of his left arm. He was warm, and it felt wonderful to be so close to him with her left hand reaching across his chest to keep the bandage in place.

"I think the bleeding's stopped. It's less, anyway."

"Good." He squeezed her shoulders lightly, pulling her closer against his side.

"Mike."

"What?"

They looked at each other. She knew she should move away or at least admonish him, but she didn't want to. They sat that way for a long moment, neither one of them moving.

"So," he said at last. "I grew up in Smith Creek, Tennessee. I had two brothers and three sisters."

"And?"

"What else do you want to know?"

"Everything."

"For a woman who intends to walk out of my life soon, you're nosy."

"No, I just thought we should put the enforced waiting period to good use."

"Ah, yes. Idle hands and all that."

"Michael, really!" She shifted so she wasn't so close to him.

"So tell me about yourself," he said.

"All right, that's fair. You know that my parents died some time ago."

"No, I didn't."

She nodded. "They did. And I went to live with my aunt, who saw to my education at Miss Clarkson's, to her ruin."

"How is that?"

"She apparently bankrupted herself to pay for my schooling."

Mike grimaced. "She mustn't have had much to begin with. Either that, or she had some bad financial advice."

"Well, however it happened, she passed away a year after my graduation, and I learned that I was destitute. Miss Clarkson helped me find this job, so here I am, out to conquer the West and civilize the children of the pioneers.

He smiled. "You'll do it, too."

"So. . .your family?"

He squinted at her in the shadows. "You want to know about Martha."

She swallowed. "Do I?"

"Don't you?"

"Perhaps I do."

He was silent for a moment, then stirred. "She was my first love. My only love. We knew each other all our lives, grew up in the same valley. It just seemed the natural thing to get married. There was no one else I ever felt close to."

"You loved her."

"Of course." He shook his head slightly, as though he didn't enjoy confronting the past. "Well, we were quite young, and I don't really have anything to compare it to, but looking back now, yes, I would say we loved each other very much." He chuckled. "There were times when I thought she hated me. She'd yell at me, and I'd yell back. But that never lasted long."

"Sounds like us." Lydia immediately wished she hadn't said that and asked hastily, "What did she look like?"

He looked toward the rock that formed the back wall of their hiding place, and his brow wrinkled as though he struggled to focus the memory.

"She wasn't at all like you."

"Is that good or bad?"

He smiled. "Her hair was pale gold. When she washed it in rainwater, it looked pretty in the sun."

Lydia kept silent, thinking how dull her own hair was after months on the dusty trail.

"She was shorter than you and thin. They never had enough to eat at their house. Her folks died when she was fifteen, and it seemed logical to get married." He looked at her suddenly, with a crooked smile. "She wasn't the independent type, and her older brothers were already married. Now, you'd do differently in that situation."

"Would I?"

"Certainly. You'd want to prove to the world that you could survive on your own. I expect you'd have stayed on in your pa's cabin alone for a while."

Lydia swallowed hard. It sounded dreadfully bleak compared to the prospect of marriage to Michael Brown. "How long were you married?"

"About five years. Billy came along a year later, and then. . . well, we lost a baby after that."

"I'm sorry."

"It happens. Martha took it hard. Then we had the fire. We had to live with my family, and that was tough, but we had absolutely nothing." His lips skewed into a grim smile. "I figured I'd enlist for a year or two and send my pay home, and then we'd be able to start over. Didn't work out that way."

Lydia pushed down the memory of the fire that had taken her father's life, but Mike's loss was more real to her because of it. "Did you miss her when you came out here?"

"Sure."

Lydia looked into his face. The carefree, teasing expression was gone, replaced by a thoughtful sorrow.

"I'm sorry you lost them, Mike."

He drew a deep breath, and she felt his lungs expand. *What am I doing?* she asked herself. *I mustn't allow myself to become attached to this man.*

But when his scratchy cheek came down gently against her forehead, she didn't resist. She let go of the bandage and hesitantly reached up to stroke his thick hair. It was cool and satiny. She closed her eyes and rested against his shoulder, unwilling to think beyond this moment to the wagon train and the weeks of trail ahead and the school in Oregon.

Suddenly Mike stiffened, and she was alert at once.

"Listen."

Far away, she heard a bugle sound and, a moment later, faint hoofbeats.

"Darlin', you'd best get out there and wave whatever's left of your underskirt so Dan Reese can find us."

seventeen

It took Reese's men only a few minutes to locate the Indians' mustangs. He assigned several troopers to carry the dead Sioux down the hillside and bury them where the ground was less rocky.

Lydia stood near where Mike was stretched out on a blanket. Mr. Paine had removed Mike's left boot and was binding his ankle while Dr. Nichols swabbed out the shoulder wound with water from his canteen.

"No way you can sit a horse all the way back to camp, Brown," Reese was saying.

"I'll make it."

"Better make a travois," Dr. Nichols said, and Reese nodded.

"Oh, wonderful." Brown scowled up at the sergeant.

"He's not a very good patient, is he?" Lydia asked.

Mike struggled to sit up, but Dr. Nichols pushed him back down. "Take it easy, would you? I'm trying to see how bad you're hurt."

"It'll mend in time. Let's get going," Mike replied.

Dr. Nichols shook his head. "You've still got the lead in your shoulder. I'm not digging it out until we get back to camp."

"It won't take long to make a travois if we can get some poles long enough," Reese said. He looked doubtfully toward the scrub pines. "Gleason, take some men and hunt up two good, straight poles."

Dr. Nichols had Mike moved into the shade. It was another half hour before the travois was ready, and in the interim Mike instructed Mr. Paine to go to the rocky cavern and gather up any unbroken arrows he could find and the short bow Lydia had left there.

"I wondered about the brave we found with an arrow

131

through his chest," Reese said, eyeing Lydia with awe.

"She saved both our necks by shooting that last one," Mike said.

Lydia sat down beside him. "Hush now. I did what I had to is all."

Mike's face was gray. His smile skewed into a grimace. "If I pass out on the trail, just make sure they get me back to camp, all right, sweetheart?"

"If you weren't hurt, I'd lambaste you."

He lay back on the blanket, smiling.

The men from the burial detail returned carrying various articles they had stripped from the Lakota. Lydia recognized Skunk's necklace and looked away. Mike stirred and eyed their plunder keenly.

"Hey, Shorty," he called.

A large private walked over to where he lay.

"That quiver goes to Miss Jackson."

"What, this?" Shorty held up an elk hide quiver with four arrows in it.

"That's right."

Lydia felt a flush infusing her cheeks. "No, really, I don't want it."

"You earned it, Miss Jackson," said Reese.

"It'll be a good conversation piece for her class in Oregon," Mike said. "She's a good horsewoman, too."

Reese nodded. "Miss Jackson, you and Nathan Paine can each keep one of the ponies. Corporal Brown can add the other three to our string."

Private Barkley escorted her to where the five mustangs were tied. "You want one of these critters, Miss Jackson?"

Lydia looked them over. "That's the one the leader rode." She indicated a stocky brown and white pinto, made garish with black painted stripes on his legs and the imprint of the warrior's hand on his shoulder. "What does all that paint mean?"

"Mostly it's to scare you. The hand means he killed an enemy in battle sometime."

She looked at the other horses. When she saw the one that was Skunk's, she turned away, her stomach suddenly squeamish. She didn't want to ride that pony again.

"I'll take the one with the black hand."

Barkley smiled. "That's fitting, Miss Jackson. You've earned the honor."

Lydia caught her breath in a little sob. "I didn't—"

"I know, miss. You weren't saying you deserve the war paint. I said it, though. You were a real soldier, and God was surely looking down on you and Mike."

❧

Thomas Miller and three other men from the wagon train rode out and met them five miles from the camp.

"We sure are glad to see you, Miss Jackson," Miller said, sweeping off his hat for a moment. "Mrs. Paine was beside herself worrying about you and the corporal."

"How's Nathan doing?" Lydia asked.

"He's in some pain, but his mother's making him as comfortable as possible."

It was past noon when they reached the wagon train. Lydia was cosseted and fussed over by Dorcas, and most of the other ladies came by as she ravenously ate her dinner.

"My dear, you'll have to give us the whole story tonight when we make camp again," Mrs. Kemp said, looking her over. Lydia flushed, wondering if that fastidious lady could tell she was not wearing a petticoat. Her ride home on the mustang had been less than modest, but all of the men had been courteous and managed not to stare at her exposed ankles. She was reconsidering her opinion of bloomer costumes, especially with the prospect of riding her new mustang.

Jean Carver leaned toward her eagerly. "Is it true that Injun wanted you for his bride?"

"More likely for his slave," Margaret Sawyer said acidly.

"Margaret!" her mother scolded, but she listened avidly for Lydia's reply.

Lydia suspected that Margaret was jealous because she was

not the one who had had an adventure and been rescued by the handsome corporal.

"I doubt he had any such designs," Lydia said evenly. "The sergeant says they might have traded me back for some horses."

Margaret smirked as though that idea was clearly a fabrication.

"There now, ladies," Dorcas said. "Mrs. Miller tells me we'll be pulling out any minute. I must pack up my dishes. Off with you."

❧

The next morning, Mike waited impatiently. He had sent Gleason to the Paines' wagon with a plea for Lydia to visit him. He wasn't at all sure she would come, but he thought he would go crazy riding in the escort's supply wagon all day. The swaying, bumping motion of the wagon sent jolts of pain through his body. There was no way he could read or otherwise occupy himself while riding in this torture chamber, except to think about Lydia.

It wasn't until the nooning stop that she climbed up over the seat of the wagon carrying a tin plate and a basket.

"Good day, Michael. I've brought you some dinner—Mrs. Paine's biscuits and some cold prairie chicken. Mr. Paine says he'll come by and see you this evening after we camp."

He struggled to sit up in spite of the searing pain it caused, and Lydia arranged the rolled up blankets he was using for pillows, to help him into a position that was nearly upright.

"There you go. I'm glad to see you looking so well. I'll come back later for the dishes."

"Don't leave," Mike said.

"I must help Dorcas. We'll be moving out soon."

He realized how long the afternoon would be riding alone in the uncomfortable wagon. "Please. I've been starving for company all morning. Tell me what's going on."

"Well, Nathan cried quite a bit this morning. He's terribly jostled. Mr. Paine spent most of the nooning trying to rig up a hammock for him inside the wagon."

"That's a good idea. I wonder if it would work in here."

Mike looked around at the crammed interior of the supply wagon.

"All of the other boys were jealous when they heard Nathan and I have Sioux ponies. They think we went off on a lark and came back with fabulous loot." Lydia smiled. "At least it took Nathan's mind off his leg for a while when Chub Hadley and Ralph Miller came by to see him. Then Private Gleason let Chub and Ralph help him take the ponies into the river to wash the war paint off."

"Which one did Nathan pick?"

"The one with the most white."

"Bad choice."

Lydia scowled at him. "He's eight years old. The boy doesn't know anything about horses yet. Just let him enjoy it. Besides, they're all healthy. If he picks the worst one, why should you care? You'll get the better ones for your remounts."

"The boy needs the one that's calmest and best behaved. That dun."

"The small one? What boy would choose the runt?"

Again Mike felt the chafing of his confinement. "When I'm on my feet again, I'll bring the extra mounts by the Paines' wagon and show him their good points. If he wants to choose another one, I'll let him."

"Mr. Paine rode the pinto before he let Nathan choose. He didn't see anything wrong with that horse."

"Fine. Josiah's not a bad judge of horseflesh. And how do you like your pony?"

"We're getting along well."

"Sit, Lydia."

Immediately her eyes darkened. "I mustn't."

"Gossip?" She didn't answer, and he gave a short sigh of disgust. "It's not like I'm in any shape to be accused of molesting you."

"Please don't speak so. I was starting to reclassify you as a gentleman, you know."

"I'm sorry. I just get so tired of these biddies. Mrs. Sawyer is the worst, and her daughters aren't any better, or so I'm told."

"By whom?"

"Ask any trooper."

"Ah, so the men of the escort gossip, as well." The corners of her tempting lips seemed to twitch.

Mike laughed. "You got me. But seriously, can't you spend ten minutes with me, the poor wounded man who rescued you?"

"You're going to use that to your advantage all the way to Oregon, aren't you?"

"I hope I won't turn into a malingering invalid," he said with a smile.

She sat down on the edge of a crate of staples, smoothing her delft blue skirt. Mike didn't think he had seen that dress before. She'd worn a green dress occasionally, but when she was captured she had been wearing her habitual mulberry dress. That one was probably ruined during the ordeal, he realized, from rough treatment and the stains of his own blood.

"I'll stay a few minutes," she said. "After that I must go help Dorcas with the children. But if you behave yourself, I'll come see you again tomorrow with breakfast. Maybe I'll bring Jenny."

"That would be nice. I should be in the saddle again in a couple of days."

"Surely your injuries won't permit that."

"We'll see."

"Yes, we shall."

She smiled, and Mike felt a pang in his heart that wasn't caused by his wound. Why did she have to take this teaching job? He didn't want to think about leaving her in Oregon and riding back over the mountains to the fort.

"Lydia, do you have to take this position?"

She blinked at him. "That's why they asked me to sign a contract, Michael. To be sure I'd honor the commitment."

He looked up at the canvas above him. The sun had beat on it all morning, and the air inside the wagon was nearly stifling. "But couldn't you explain to them. . ."

Lydia rearranged the folds of her skirt unnecessarily and smoothed down a wrinkle. He could tell by the set of her mouth that she wouldn't seriously consider backing out on the arrangement. "They've lost a lot of prospective teachers to marriage out here. The school board thought it best to have me sign a very rigid agreement before they advanced me the money for my train ticket to Independence and my expenses for the trip."

Mike sighed. Money had changed hands, and it was clear Lydia saw this as a matter of honor. "You've prayed about all this, I suppose."

"For many months now. Michael, I must keep my word."

"I can see that. I'm sorry I urged you not to. I didn't realize how binding it was." Mike lay back on the blankets.

"Your bandages should be changed," she said.

He looked down. She was right; blood was oozing through the bandage on his shoulder. He smiled at her. "I hope you won't find it necessary to sacrifice any more of your wardrobe for me."

She darted a cool glance at him, but her reply was indulgent. "The doctor will take care of it, I'm sure."

Pain from the wound still stabbed him with each breath, and his ankle throbbed, but he was able to ignore the discomfort while he considered his future with Lydia, or the impossibility of one. Dr. Nichols had said that morning that he expected the injuries to heal well, so they were the least of Mike's worries.

"He said he'd come by and tend to it after he sees Mrs. Sawyer and Nathan," Mike admitted.

"Did he give you anything for the pain?"

"He offered me laudanum, but I turned him down. I don't want to be rendered senseless for a flesh wound."

She picked up the basket. "Really, Michael, there's nothing more to say about my employment. I'm going to teach this fall. I feel God would have me do this."

"Wait!" He struggled to sit up as she stood. "Lydia, you know I care about you. If it weren't for that contract, I'd be on my knees begging you to marry me."

She pressed her lips firmly together, and her eyes glistened with unshed tears. "Thank you. I shall always remember that. Good day, sir."

"A few moments ago you were calling me Michael."

She avoided his piercing stare once more. "I came here as a friend. We went through a lot together in the last couple of days. But this must be the extent of it. You understand."

He sank back. "I'm sorry. And I'm sorry for all the times I made you angry. Forgive me, Lydia."

She smiled at his contrition. "Of course. That's part of life, Corporal, when two strong-willed people cross paths. But that's what this has been. We met, we travel along together for a few months, and then we part."

❧

That night, Lydia lay awake for hours. The knowledge that Mike loved her and would gladly have married her was sweet and painful. But no matter how she turned the issue around in her mind, she knew that she couldn't give up the teaching job and ride back to Fort Laramie with the escort.

She sighed and rolled over. Would the image of handsome, laughing Mike Brown haunt her dreams for the rest of her life? Would this be the one huge regret she fostered? Or would God bring some other man into her life later on when she was free of her obligation to the school board? Lydia rejected that idea immediately. She would never love this deeply again. Surely she couldn't feel the same way when another man kissed her as she had when Mike did. She should never have allowed him to touch her in the rocky cavern, as glorious as that one kiss had been. The memory would spoil any other man's chances of winning her affections.

It was confusing, and she rolled over again, hoping to find a comfortable spot on the ground and drift off to sleep, but slumber eluded her.

She stared up at the brilliant stars. *Lord, I'm sorry. I was foolish to let myself care for Michael. Please forgive me, and help me not to let this affect my ability as a teacher. I truly want to do a good job, to please the parents, and to help the children love learning.*

She took a deep, shuddering breath. *Help me to be true to my promise, Lord. I know it's the right thing, and I must honor my word.*

She sighed and followed the two pointer stars of the Big Dipper up the black velvet sky to the gleaming North Star. It was easy. As usual, Mike was right.

eighteen

Mike waited restlessly for Lydia the next morning. He was afraid she wouldn't come, and it nearly drove him to action, but when he tried to stand, he realized he was very weak from loss of blood and sank back, breathing deeply and berating himself.

He could smell food cooking outside, but still she didn't come. Cattle were hustled to their places to be yoked, and mules were harnessed. His stomach rumbled. He was very hungry, but no one brought him anything to eat.

He was thoroughly exasperated by the time the sergeant poked his head in.

"How you doing, Mike?"

"I'm starving to death. Thought you forgot about me."

"No, Miss Jackson said she'd bring you something before we head out. She hasn't been here?"

"No, she has not."

"We're nearly ready to move. Need some help this morning?"

"I want to shave."

Reese frowned. "No time, Mike. Maybe Miss Jackson will help you when we stop for nooning."

"I don't want Miss Jackson to help me. I can shave myself. Just fetch me my razor and some soap."

"We're going to start moving. You'd cut your throat. But I'll send Gleason in to help you dress."

The wagon gave a lurch and started rolling ten minutes later, after Gleason had left him reasonably comfortable but still feeling scruffy. Mike was sure Lydia had forgotten him and he would go hungry until noon.

But before they had fallen into the rhythm of movement, she scrambled up over the wagon seat, juggling a coffeepot and a basket.

"I'm sorry. Jenny was fussy this morning, and Mrs. Paine is afraid she has a fever. I had to cook breakfast and pack up everything."

"It's all right." Mike felt hypocritical as he spoke. "You don't have to do this. One of the troopers could have brought me breakfast."

"Well, I said I would do it, and I always try to keep my word. I just didn't realize how hectic things would be at the Paine camp this morning."

She was removing items from the basket, and Mike sat up eagerly as she lifted the inverted tin plate that covered his breakfast. The smell of the golden griddle cakes and bacon was enough to drive a man wild.

"You're feeling better."

"I am. I feel as if I could do some scouting after a good breakfast."

Lydia frowned as she rummaged for a fork. "You take it easy. I'm afraid your food's cooled off. I left the coffee on the hot rocks 'til the last second. It should be piping hot." She poured a tin cup half full and offered it cautiously as the wagon rolled forward.

Mike held it carefully, hoping the mules pulling the wagon wouldn't lurch into a rut while he asked a blessing for his meal. After a few seconds of heartfelt prayer, he opened his eyes to find Lydia watching him unabashed.

"Lydia, I've given your situation a lot of thought, and I can see that you're right. Please forgive me for suggesting that you break your contract. That was wrong."

She shrugged. "Everyone gets a little excitable when discussing a sensitive topic. That's partly why I wanted to see you today. To be sure you know I'm settled in my mind. I think God would have me fulfill my promise."

"Yes, I see that now." He began to eat, and the food was a comfort to his empty stomach, but his spirits had reached a new low. Lydia would not change her mind, which was as it should be, but it did not ease his grief. He drained the tin cup and set it down. "I appreciate you bringing me this delicious breakfast, but don't feel obligated to keep coddling me. If you'd rather not come again. . ."

She shook her head with impatience. "This is not penance, Michael. You're a friend to me and the Paines. And after all, you did save my life."

"You would have survived."

"Perhaps, but the prospect of survival with the Sioux is not one I want to contemplate."

He knew the terror of her capture would be with her a long time and decided that with a spirited girl like Lydia it might be best to make light of it. "They would have treated you like a princess once they were safe in their village. It wouldn't have been long before one of those Lakota braves dropped a deer carcass in front of your teepee."

Her eyes widened. "I assume you're saying one of them would court me."

"That's what they do. It sort of proves he could support you, feed your family."

She shuddered. "I don't think Skunk was worried about courtship rituals."

He pressed his lips together. Wrong tactic. "This was a fine breakfast, Lydia. Thank you."

"Was it enough? I had to douse the fire and—"

"It's plenty." They sat looking at each other in the shade of the wagon cover. A little frown wrinkled Lydia's forehead.

"I'm sorry," he said at last.

"For what?"

"I can't help loving you, but I shouldn't have pressed you on that score. You've made a pledge."

"Yes," she whispered. "It's one thing my father taught me very young. You don't go back on your word." She began packing the dishes in the basket. "Would you like more coffee? There's a little left."

"Thank you."

As she poured it, he regretted not saying no and just letting her go. She was unsettled again. It seemed to happen every time they were together, and he didn't know how to change that.

"You were wonderful through the whole ordeal, you know," he said at last.

"No. I was terrified. If you and Mr. Paine hadn't come. . ." She straightened suddenly and faced him. "Look, Michael, I know we became very close out there in the wilderness. I'm not sorry about that. You were the one man I was longing to see, and since I had to go through all that, I'm glad it was with you. But that doesn't mean. . ."

She stopped, and he thought she was blushing as she reached for the coffeepot and thrust it into the basket.

"I shouldn't have kissed you."

She sat very still. "Perhaps not." Her voice was very small.

He waited, but she didn't acknowledge that she had kissed him back and had made no complaints at the time. The tenderness and desire that filled his heart was overwhelming, and he reached for her hand.

"Lydia, dearest Lydia, I'm not sorry that I love you or that I kissed you, only that it's bothering you now. I never expected this to happen, to fall in love again. And I had no idea you were obligated to a life that can't include me. If it weren't for the promise you made many months ago—"

"But I did!" She jumped up and seized the basket, backing away from him. "I can't break my promise, Michael. I've gone round and round with the Lord about this, and I truly feel He would have me keep my pledge."

Mike sighed. "Of course. You're right, and I won't speak to you of this again."

She stared at him for a long moment, then nodded. "Very well. I think that's best. You should rest now."

"Psalm 15, darlin'."

"I beg your pardon?"

Mike reached for his battered Psalter and winced. "Do you have a Bible?"

"Yes."

"Psalm 15. I was looking at it this morning, and it helped me to understand that what you're doing is right. It may help you, too."

⅋

Lydia hurried back to the Paines' wagon, her blue skirt swirling about her ankles. She had worn it this morning to help her decide whether or not to alter it. All of the Sawyer girls, and even Frances, were dividing their long skirts into billowy trousers. Frances wore hers under another skirt. As much as the fashion had shocked her at first, Lydia knew that if she wanted to spend much time riding the Lakota pony, she would have to adopt the frontier mode.

The blue dress was her favorite, and she had been saving it in the bottom of her carpetbag so that she would have one fresh outfit when she reached her destination. She had loaned it to Minnie Carver for a night of dancing but had not worn it herself on the trip until today.

Now, with Oregon City still two months away, that seemed shortsighted. The prospect of riding the sturdy pinto was enticing, and she knew as she climbed up on the wagon seat beside Dorcas, pausing to lift her cumbersome skirt, that she would be wearing bloomers before the week was out. She winced at the pain in her bruised hip. It had plagued her since she fell from the Indian's pony, but it wasn't bad enough to worry about.

"How's Jenny?" she asked.

Dorcas sighed. "Sleeping at last. I laid her down beside Nathan."

Lydia bent to peer into the wagon. Nathan was watching her from his hammock, and she smiled and waved at him.

"Hey! Would you like me to read to you later?"

Nathan nodded. His face was pale, and Lydia was sure he was holding back tears.

"He'd like that," Dorcas said. "This jostling is hard on him."

Lydia turned to assess her friend and saw that the lines around Dorcas's eyes and mouth had deepened since Nathan's adventure. "You're exhausted. You should lie down, too. Mr.

Paine will keep the oxen going."

"There's no more room in there," Dorcas said, raising one hand in futility. "I'll be all right."

"Well, if Jenny wakes up fussy, I'll be the one to tend her."

They rode in silence for a few minutes.

"How's Corporal Brown doing?" Dorcas asked.

Lydia bit her lip, considering on what level she would answer that question. "He seems to be doing better. He's dressed, and he sat up to eat. I think he still has a lot of pain, though."

"Mm-hmm."

Lydia eyed her uneasily. Dorcas definitely had something on her mind.

"I'm going to split this skirt," she said, hoping to draw her hostess off into a discussion of fashion. Anything was preferable to discussing her feelings for Mike Brown.

"It's so pretty."

"Thank you, but I've got to do something."

"So you can ride the horse modestly?" Dorcas nodded in approval. "Perhaps you can salvage the maroon one."

"I don't know. The stains will never come out."

"But you might be able to hide them in the folds."

Lydia frowned. "You may be right. Maybe I should practice on that and keep this one for best. Still, I don't know how modest it will be. It's a bit scandalous to think I can ride astride. Back in Hartford, that would be socially reprehensible."

"Really, dear."

"Oh, yes. Ladies might ride sidesaddle for exercise occasionally but never astride. But out here, it seems to be accepted, and—"

"Why did you not tell me your teaching position would prevent you from accepting the marriage proposal of one of the finest men on earth?"

The sudden question threw Lydia off guard, and she checked for an instant, then went on. "No one seems to care if a woman wears bloomers or— Oh, Dorcas, what have I done?"

Her tears came so quickly, it shocked her, and she sobbed, burying her face in her hands. Dorcas's gentle fingers smoothed her hair, and Lydia was drawn into her kind embrace.

"How did you know?" Lydia sobbed.

"Mr. Paine visited the corporal last evening. He thought Brown might have trouble sleeping, and he was right, but it seems it wasn't because of his injuries. He's pining for you, my dear, because you've gone and pledged yourself to a career as a schoolmarm." Dorcas pushed a frayed but dainty handkerchief into her hand, and Lydia mopped her cheeks.

"Oh, Dorcas, please, you mustn't tell anyone I turned Mike down. It's almost a relief that you and Mr. Paine know, but I'd be mortified if the whole wagon train was talking about it."

Dorcas turned to look ahead over the broad backs of the oxen, and Lydia was filled with remorse.

"I'm sorry now I didn't tell you. You and Mr. Paine have been so good to me! And if Mr. Paine and Corporal Brown hadn't come after us right away, Nathan and I might be sitting at a Sioux campfire right now."

"That's neither here nor there," Dorcas said, but her face softened and she sat a little straighter. "Lydia, I've come to love you like a sister."

Lydia nodded. "That's true, and I should have known I could trust you. And Dorcas—"

"What, child?"

"I've never had a sister. It's nice that you feel that way. If I did have a real sister, I'd want her to be just like you."

She saw a tear glitter on Dorcas's lashes. Lydia reached toward her and hugged her tight for a moment.

"Thank you, dear. That's very sweet," Dorcas said softly. "If we're sisters, then perhaps you'd like to know a family secret."

Lydia leaned back and looked at her.

"An auntish sort of secret," Dorcas said.

Lydia gasped. "Do you mean there will be a new baby in the Paine family soon?"

"Not very soon, but next winter if all goes well."

Lydia squeezed her fiercely. "And I won't get to see him!"

"It will be very hard for me to leave you when we get to

Oregon. I expect everyone will know by then. I won't be able to hide it."

"Dear Dorcas, you mustn't fret. God will take care of me. And God and Mr. Paine will take care of you! He won't let you do any heavy work. And all the troopers adore you. They'll stand in line to fetch your water. Have you told Mr. Paine?"

"Oh, yes. He's very good about these things." Dorcas flushed a becoming pink. "We've lost two wee ones, you know, between Nathan and Jenny."

Lydia shook her head. "I had no idea. How ever did you stand it?"

"God knows what's best."

Lydia felt naive. She'd been so involved with her own concerns that she hadn't given much thought to uncomplaining Dorcas's situation. "But this trip is so strenuous! The sergeant says we'll have some very difficult slopes to maneuver in the Blue Mountains next month. Will you be all right?"

"I think so. I hope so." Dorcas smiled at her. "I feel well this time. Perhaps the exercise and fresh air have strengthened me. Now you must get your bonnet before the sun gets any stronger. And you mustn't be angry with Corporal Brown for divulging your secret. Mr. Paine said the corporal told him about your rejection of him in confidence."

"I'm not angry with him. Did Mr. Paine say anything else?" Lydia asked carefully, examining the edging on the crumpled handkerchief.

Dorcas squeezed her arm. "Only that his friend is feeling quite dejected just now."

"I told Michael yesterday I would take Jenny around to see him, but if she's ill, we'd better keep her away."

"Yes. You'll have to go alone, I'm afraid."

"No. No, I shan't visit him anymore. There's no point in spending time with him when nothing can come of it."

Dorcas inhaled deeply. "Just so. I expect he'll be up and around soon, anyway."

nineteen

Jenny was still fretful that evening, and Lydia and Dorcas took turns holding her, but the little girl seemed to have lost her fever. Nathan begged Lydia for story after story. Lydia attempted to keep him occupied and also do the chores he would have done if he were healthy. At last, when the dishes were done, the fuel and water in place for morning, and both children asleep, she was able to bring out her Bible and sit down with it beside the wagon wheel. It was still too hot to sit near the fire, and they had let it die out after supper.

She leafed to the Psalms, her heart pounding as she recalled Mike's words. What message was he giving her?

The Psalm consisted of only five verses, and in the fading light she read with increasing curiosity the passage that described a righteous man. What did Mike mean? It was the end of verse 4 that stopped her, and warm recognition flooded her. "He honoureth them that fear the Lord. He that sweareth to his own hurt, and changeth not."

She leaned back against the wagon wheel for a long time, letting the twilight settle around her. At first the sky was dark. Then all at once, she could see a handful of stars. The Big Dipper leaped out, and she wondered why she'd never been able to find it before, it was so prominent in the sky to the north.

Lord, is that what I've done, sworn to my own hurt?

It hadn't seemed so. Back in Connecticut, she'd been certain the job offer was God's answer to her many prayers for guidance. The Lord would honor her for keeping the promise. That was Mike's message to her. It wrenched her heart to realize he was suffering as he watched her try to do right.

The Paines came from the river path, and Dorcas picked up the cooling coffeepot.

"Let me do that," Lydia said, rising quickly.

Dorcas glanced toward her Bible. "You're in the middle of a conversation, I'd say."

"I think we've finished for now. I'll fill the coffeepot for breakfast and put these things away. You go ahead and retire, Dorcas. It's been a long day for you, and Jenny's quiet now. Take advantage of that."

"Howdy, folks." They all turned toward the voice. Trooper Gleason sauntered toward them. His gaze settled on Lydia. "Evening, Miss Jackson."

"Hello," Lydia said, and the Paines greeted him.

"I'm on an errand of mercy for Corporal Brown." Gleason smiled amiably. "He's getting a bit fidgety. Nichols just told him he can't get out of bed for at least two more days, and he's fretful, so I'm making the rounds to see if anyone's got some reading material to occupy him tomorrow."

"Haven't got any books," Dorcas said. "Just the Bible."

"Mike's a big reader, is he?" Paine asked.

"Oh, yes, sir. Whenever we get a new book at the fort, he's always eager to get his hands on it."

"I'm sorry we can't help you," Dorcas said. "Books are too heavy to cart up and down these mountains."

"Yes, ma'am, I agree with you there," Gleason said.

"I have a few small volumes," Lydia said.

The trooper's grin was triumphant. "There, now. I told Mike you'd have something for him."

"Of course!" said Dorcas. "Miss Jackson plans to be a school-teacher, you know."

"Don't surprise me none," Gleason said with a smile. "You speak so proper and all."

Lydia went to the back of the wagon, opened her little trunk, and chose two slim books. Gleason peered at them in the twilight, frowning. "Well, I'm sure he'll be grateful, miss. I'll bring them back when he's done."

"I'll do up these few chores," Lydia said to Dorcas.

"Thank you," Dorcas replied. "Good night, Private Gleason."

Mr. Paine nodded at the trooper and ambled off to check his livestock.

"Mind if I set a spell?" Gleason asked.

Lydia tried to think of an excuse to turn him away. "I—"

"You seem to be fully recovered from your misadventure." Gleason grinned as he settled down on the crate Mr. Paine used as his stool for meals.

Lydia considered that. "I suppose I'm none the worse physically. I wish I could take some of the pain for Nathan."

"How's the boy doing?"

"He's miserable. Cries a lot."

"That's sure a shame."

"Yes. He's a brave little boy, but unrelieved torment wears on the best of us."

Gleason nodded. "That's for sure. Mike Brown's grouchy as a grizzly bear."

"He seemed to be doing better this morning."

"Oh, he is. That's half the problem. He wants to get on a horse, and the sergeant won't let him."

"He'll heal quickly." She stowed the last of the supper things in a wooden box and started to pick it up.

Gleason jumped up. "Allow me."

"Thank you. I was just going to set it under the corner of the wagon there."

He deposited the crate where she indicated, then turned to her expectantly. "I'd be honored if you'd stroll with me, Miss Jackson."

"Oh, no, thank you. I'm very tired." She untied her apron and began to fold it.

His disappointment was evident. "Of course. I just wanted a chance to tell you how much we fellows admire you and the way you got out of that scrape with the Sioux."

Lydia tried not to let her confusion show. The last thing she wanted was to be admired for killing a man. "I do hope the troopers aren't making large of the incident. After all, I was foolish enough to get into the predicament in the first place."

He grinned. "Most of us think you'd be just the woman that a man would want to have beside him. Of course, there's a few who pretend they'd be afraid to be alone with you."

"Oh, really?"

"They're just joshing. They don't mean anything by it."

"I wish the men wouldn't talk about me."

His pale eyebrows arched. "Why, that's impossible, Miss Jackson. Your narrow escape is a wonder, and until something more sensational happens, folks are bound to talk about it."

"I suppose so. We're like a small village here."

"Exactly. Sergeant Reese says you're a heroine, and the corporal would have been done for if you hadn't of skewered that Injun."

"Excuse me, please." Lydia turned away, feeling a little queasy. The macabre image of Skunk's body was still vivid in her mind—his sightless eyes staring at nothing in the first rays of dawn, a smear of blood darkening his cheek. She turned toward the wagon.

"Evening, miss," another male voice called, and Lydia turned back to greet the newcomer.

It was Dr. Nichols, carrying a small bag. "Thought I'd check on the boy."

"He's resting," Lydia said.

"Good. The willow bark tea's doing some good, then."

"It soothes him for a while."

Dr. Nichols nodded. "Well, tell his mother I said to give him a little of that laudanum if he needs it in the night. Not too much. I told her the dose."

"Thank you. I will."

Dr. Nichols smiled. "I'll come back in the morning, then. But Mr. Paine can fetch me in the night if he needs to. Don't want the boy thrashing about."

Dr. Nichols left, and Gleason smiled sadly at her.

"Good night, then."

"Good night."

Gleason followed the doctor, carrying the books. Lydia

took a deep breath and let it out in a sigh before she took her blanket roll down from the wagon. Nathan's uneven breathing told her that the boy slept fitfully. She hoped the medicine would give him enough relief that he wouldn't wake the family and all their neighbors with his crying, the way he had for the last two nights.

Her troubled thoughts plagued her as she prepared for bed. Maybe it would be better if she let it be known in the camp that she was not open to receiving suitors. Maybe then the troopers would stop talking about her, and Gleason would give up trying to woo her.

She shuddered at the thought of keeping company with John Gleason. He was a nice enough fellow, but his indelicacy repelled her. She supposed he wasn't bad-looking, but beside Corporal Brown, he was clumsy and insipid. And even though Brown had been reared in a remote Appalachian valley, his education was broader than that of most of the men. Apparently he was an insatiable reader and had educated himself. That was important to her in a man. One who couldn't think deeply held no attraction for her. And Mike had a way of taking things he had read and fitting them into the world he lived in.

She caught herself up sharply. How had she gone from her dislike of Gleason to admiration for Brown? She wouldn't allow her thoughts to take that direction. No more pining over a man she couldn't have. She would think instead about her students and the lessons she would prepare for them.

She shook out her bedroll with the bleak realization that she could have faced spinsterhood more cheerfully if she had not tasted love.

❧

Lydia saw Mike again three days later from a distance. He was riding a calm, rather swaybacked mule. The toes of his left boot barely touched the stirrup, but he was in the saddle and apparently attempting to resume his duties.

He didn't come around the Paines' wagon, but a few days later, when they were well on their way northward toward the Snake River, Mr. Paine brought back her Tennyson and slipped it into her hands without comment.

Lydia carried it with her that day as she walked, leafing through it, wondering which of the poems had caught Mike's interest. She had marked "Maud" with a pencil when she first read it because the lyrical cadence had thrilled her. She flushed as she wondered if Mike had noticed the slash beside the title and drawn any inferences from that.

There was a small stain on the page with "Charge of the Light Brigade," and she wondered if Mike had spilled his coffee on it as the wagon lurched.

"While horse and hero fell, they that had fought so well came through the jaws of Death. . ." Yes, Mike would relate to that poem. She wondered what he would make of her Oliver Wendell Holmes.

Frances came to walk with her. They took Jenny and Frances's younger sister, Rachel, with them. It wasn't long before Margaret and Eliza Sawyer joined them.

"Charlie's talking of leaving us," Margaret announced.

"Why?" asked Frances.

"Because of Ellen. She won't give him the time of day anymore. Charlie's furious. He says he's going back to Fort Bridger and see if the Pony Express will take him. If not, he might head up north and join the argonauts."

"Gold hunting?" Frances gasped.

Margaret shrugged. "He just wants to get away. That and he wants adventure, I guess."

"Isn't this journey adventure enough?" Lydia asked.

"Well, maybe if he'd gotten to chase the Sioux that captured you he'd be content." Margaret's exasperated tone surprised Lydia. "There's a whole lot of young fellows who wish they were in Corporal Brown's boots, I'll tell you."

"That's crazy," Lydia said. "The man was almost killed, and he's suffering terribly now."

"Tim and Charlie don't see it that way," Frances told her. "Brown lay low for a few days, but he's on scout duty again and looking none the worse for wear."

"He hasn't fully recovered," Lydia insisted.

"Makes no difference to them. It wouldn't surprise me if every young man on this train joined the cavalry because of Corporal Brown and his derring-do."

"Well, that might be better than having them go off up the Snake for gold," Lydia said.

Margaret shook her head. "All the troopers got to gallop off to rescue you, and the boys had to stay here and guard us and the livestock for nothing."

Lydia winced. "So all the men in the wagon train are discontented, and it's my fault."

"I'm sorry." Frances grabbed her hand. "We're making too much of this."

"I don't know," Margaret said sharply. "You've got a perfectly gorgeous man eating out of your hand, and you ignore him."

Lydia stopped walking. "What on earth—"

"Lydia, everyone's talking about how shabbily you've treated the corporal."

"That can't be true."

Margaret raised her eyebrows. "Whether it's true or not, I don't know, but they're saying it."

"You know I didn't mean it that way."

Frances sighed. "Yes, Margaret. You're not being kind."

"But why would folks think there was anything between the corporal and me?" Lydia was fairly certain Dorcas had kept her promise and not discussed her secret with anyone else, but she might have let something slip.

"He used to hang about the Paines' wagon," Margaret said.

"He and Mr. Paine are friends. And anyway, he hasn't come around at all since—since before the incident in question."

Margaret sniffed. "Minnie Carver saw you walking with him before that. She said he was holding your hand."

"That was courtesy," Lydia said weakly.

"Margaret, do be quiet," Frances begged. She turned to Lydia. "It's just. . .well, everyone knows Brown saved your life, and it seems you hardly speak to him. People assume something happened between you."

"Yes," said Margaret. "Did something happen out there? Was he shockingly forward?"

"No, he was very polite."

"Well then, what kind of woman are you?"

It hurt to inhale. Lydia swallowed hard. "Should I throw myself at a man because he helped me? I assure you, I've conveyed my sincere thanks to Corporal Brown."

Frances looked very uncomfortable. "Forgive us. I know you wouldn't snub anyone who made a sacrifice like that for you. Some folks assume Brown is enamored of you, and apparently it's not so."

Margaret's face was more skeptical.

Lydia wanted badly to tell Frances the truth, but with Margaret standing there, she knew she couldn't. Every scrap of conversation Margaret heard would be front-page news throughout the train by suppertime. She would have to keep Dorcas as her only true confidante.

Lydia looked at Margaret. "Next time someone tells you what an inhumane monster I am, please squelch the rumors by telling the truth. Corporal Brown is a true gentleman. We shared a harrowing experience, but that is all. When this train reaches Oregon City, I expect the corporal and I will never see one another again."

twenty

Lydia hoped she would have a chance to speak to Mike, but all week he flitted out of camp at dawn and returned at suppertime, never coming near the Paines' wagon.

As the sun lowered in the west on Saturday, she went to gather up the laundry she had spread earlier to dry on the grass. She was startled when Mike rode up to her on the bay mare.

"May I help you?" he asked.

She straightened, unsure what her response should be and conscious of a riotous gladness.

"You must be feeling better."

"Ninety percent, I'd say." He grimaced as he dismounted but faced her with a grin. "Are you in the talking vein, as 'The Autocrat of the Breakfast Table' would say?"

"Oh, you've been reading Holmes." She smiled and folded one of Dorcas's dish towels.

"Never laughed so hard in my life. I'll have it back to you soon, but I'm enjoying it immensely."

Lydia looked toward the wagons, wondering how many people were watching them. "You're putting your reputation at risk by talking to me."

"I'll take the chance."

Lydia sobered. "You really shouldn't."

"Has it been so bad as all that for you? Josiah told me you were upset over the gossip."

"Aren't you?"

"No, I just laugh it off. I told the fellows in my detachment that you're not nearly as haughty as some are making you out to be, that you're actually a pleasant companion and a good scout to have along when things are tough. So if they inundate you with invitations to dance tonight, I suppose it's my fault."

"But Margaret thinks—"

Mike laughed. "Margaret tried to dress me down a few days ago for flirting with you when we were off alone together. I put on a woebegone face and told her quite sadly that I had no idea what she was talking about and that I never learned to flirt. It just isn't done in Tennessee. I think she half believed me."

"That won't last. She'll be after you, trying to get you to flirt outrageously so she can prove you lied."

"Ha! That won't go over. I'm leaving soon."

"Scouting?"

"Yes, Barkley and I are going ahead, all the way to Fort Dalles. We'll be gone a couple of weeks, I expect. We heard there was a lot of rain in the Blue Mountains, and Reese wants a full report on the trail between here and the Columbia."

Lydia caught her breath. "Should you be riding so much? It's too soon."

"I thought you were a great proponent of physical exercise."

"Not while you're convalescing."

"I'll be fine."

She thought he looked too thin and his eyes had lost their glint, but she didn't say so. "When are you leaving?"

"First light."

A bleak loneliness settled over her. She would miss him, but she couldn't say that.

Mike smiled. "Don't fret about us. We'll be back in time to help you over the mountains. We'll need every man for that."

"Keep safe, Mike."

He nodded and looked into her eyes for one sober moment. "You, too. And stick to your guns. This is what God wants you to do."

"I will." She felt her face flushing.

Mike handed her the last of the laundry and put his hand to the brim of his hat. "All right, then. I hope I haven't caused you any trouble by speaking to you. I'll see you in two or three weeks."

The wagons were already climbing the lower slopes of the Blue Mountains when Brown and Barkley returned from their mission. They were out of hostile Indian territory, so there was less tension in the camp.

The trail was rougher than Lydia had anticipated. She'd assumed they had passed the worst of it, but the mountains that stood between them and their goal were fierce guardians. Sergeant Reese assured the travelers that the trail was much improved since the days of the first wagon trains. Even so, as they wound their way up from the plain, the wagons were tested, and several had to stop for repairs. One crashed down a steep incline and had to be abandoned. The owners salvaged their clothing, tools, and what supplies weren't scattered, and used their two surviving mules as pack animals.

Private Wilson and Sergeant Reese helped the Paines get their wagon down safely, and Lydia occasionally glimpsed Mike going from one family to another to aid them. She noticed that Mike limped when on foot. He was working too hard too soon, she had no doubt. She tried not to worry about his health. Instead she focused on the future, asking God to prepare her for what lay ahead.

Private Barkley came by the Paines' campsite one evening. They were perched on the side of a steep slope. Reese and Miller had hoped to reach the valley floor that day but decided camping on a slant was preferable to navigating at dusk.

"Did you see any Indians on your scouting trip?" Mr. Paine asked Barkley.

Lydia listened while she stirred up bread dough to set for the night. If she rose early, she could bake it before they broke camp.

"Just a few, and that was back near the Snake River. We ran into a band of Nez Perce. They have the most gorgeous horses! Some are spotted all over, and some just on the hindquarters. They're sweet-natured, and they run like the wind!"

"Better than those scrub mustangs the Sioux were using?" Paine asked.

"Sir, you wouldn't believe it! Those horses could sweep any racetrack in the East. And they're pleasing to the eye."

"They certainly made an impression on you." Mr. Paine lifted the coffeepot. "Cup of coffee, Barkley?"

"Thanks! Mike and I are planning to go back there next summer."

"Up the Snake River?"

"That's right. My brother's starting a horse ranch down near Fort Bridger, and he's always looking for good stock. I don't think he'll find any better than those Palouse horses. Mike thought we could convince T. R. to go up there with us after spring planting."

Lydia spread a linen towel over her bread pan and placed it on a warm rock at the edge of the fire pit. So Mike was done grieving over their love. She could almost picture him laughing about it with Barkley as they rode the trail together. "Oh, well, she gave me the mitten. Can't do anything about it." Now he was making plans for the future that didn't include her.

She went to where Dorcas was holding Jenny. "Let me get her ready for bed. She's half asleep already."

Dorcas passed the baby to her and scanned Lydia's face. "Is anything wrong?"

Lydia smiled. "No. Just feeling sorry for myself. The trip is nearly over, and I shall miss you all."

"Perhaps you'll be close enough to visit us now and then."

"Perhaps."

Dorcas patted her arm. "You're young, dear. You'll have a family of your own one day."

Lydia drew a deep breath. "Am I that transparent?"

"You'll make a fine teacher. And someday, I've no doubt you'll make a fine wife and mother."

"Thank you. That is my prayer."

With a nod, Dorcas said, "Mr. Paine and I shall continue to pray to that end."

❧

Mike was relieved when all the wagons were down the western side of the mountains. There was a good enough trail by land to Oregon City now. No more rafting down the Columbia, the way folks had done in the old days. A few families had already left the train to set off on their own, but most were heading for the land office in Oregon City to claim a piece of property.

The escort would sell its mule teams and wagons there and buy supplies for their return trip. They would ride back quickly, getting over the mountains again before the snows set in. Mike couldn't say he looked forward to it. Ordinarily he would have been glad to see the detail ended and head back to the fort and the familiar routine. But that would mean leaving Lydia behind forever.

He tossed the dregs of his coffee onto the ground. Time to check the animals before turning in.

Josiah Paine met him near the picket line, and Mike smiled. He would regret leaving the Paines, too. He'd kept away from their camp for more than a month now to avoid causing Lydia further embarrassment, but he and Josiah often spent an evening together.

"How you holding up, Mike?" Josiah asked.

"A mite stiff, but otherwise all right."

As they made the rounds of the animals, Mike checked the cavalry's mules and horses.

"Not long until we part ways," Paine said.

The big mule, Buster, stretched his neck to nuzzle Mike's shirt, and Mike scratched his forehead. "How's Lydia?"

"She's quiet. Spends a lot of time reading to Nathan."

"The boy ought to be up and about soon."

"Doc Nichols says give it another week. Don't want to take a chance on him breaking the bone again now."

"It still pains him?"

"Not so much. He says it itches a lot. Dorcas rubs it with grease every evening."

Mike sighed and looked up at the sky. "I'll miss your family.

Makes me want to go civilian again. Start a family all over." He shook his head. "But we both know that's not about to happen."

"You're staying with the army, then?"

Mike shrugged. "I don't know. I got to thinking about mustering out in December, but. . .I just don't know. My first family is gone. I didn't envision starting a new one. Does God give a man a second chance on something like that?"

"Sometimes."

"If I'd met Lydia under different circumstances. . ."

Josiah reached out to pat one of the horses. "You sound like it's now or never, Mike."

"She won't have me."

"That's today. It doesn't necessarily mean forever."

Mike stared at him. He had taken Lydia's declaration as final, and somehow he was unable to let the ashes of hope rekindle.

"She sets a lot of store by you," Josiah said.

They walked on, past the end of the picket line and onto the prairie. Mike had no fear of hostile Indians in this area. It felt good to be out away from the sounds and smells of the camp.

"If only she hadn't signed that paper," Mike murmured.

"I don't see it quite that way."

"No?"

Josiah shook his head. "The way she tells it, she was penniless. She prayed for a solution to her plight, and God gave her this. Mike, if she hadn't gotten the job offer, you never would have met her."

"No, I s'pose not."

"You and Lydia, when you're not scrapping, make quite a team."

"Always pulling in opposite directions." Mike's ankle began to ache, and he favored it slightly. He turned in a wide arc, heading back toward the wagons.

"Be thankful the Lord put her here on this train and you had the chance to see the stuff she's made of."

"You mean. . .when the Sioux took her?"

"Yes. Could you ask for a woman to acquit herself better?"

"No. I love her pluck, even her stubbornness. She never gives up."

"There you go. Be glad she wants to stick to her promise."

"That's an admirable trait, isn't it?" Mike looked at Josiah in the moonlight.

"Well, sure. If she'd made a promise to you, you'd want her to keep it."

"Naturally."

"I've said it before: Bide your time, Mike."

"I expect that's good advice."

❧

They approached Oregon City three weeks later. Lydia was restless, alternately eager and depressed. They camped three miles from town one clear night in early September, and everyone bustled about, preparing for the big day.

When they sat down for their last supper together beside the wagon, Mr. Paine offered the blessing, then said to Lydia, "We'll take you to meet the school board chairman tomorrow afternoon, once I've filed the paperwork at the land office."

"Oh, you needn't do that," Lydia said as she dished out the stew.

"Nonsense." Dorcas added a biscuit to each tin plate and handed the children their portions. "We wouldn't think of doing otherwise."

Lydia felt tears rising, and she brushed them away with the hem of her apron. "You've been most kind to me. I shall always think of you as my family."

"That suits us just fine," said Dorcas.

Her husband smiled. "So long as we don't cause you any 'Paine.'"

Lydia laughed. "On the contrary, you've chased away many of my aches on this journey."

"Well, Mr. Paine and I have agreed, and we hope you will, too, that if at all possible, you'll come and spend Christmas with us." Dorcas sat down and pulled Jenny onto her lap, balancing the child's plate just within her reach.

"We'll read stories and play games," Nathan said.

"And eat Christmas pudding," added Mr. Paine.

"Now I am going to cry." Lydia favored them all with a watery smile.

Mr. Paine looked beyond her, then smiled and started to rise. "Mike! Just in time for supper."

Mike stepped into the family circle. "Thanks, but I had a bite at the escort's fire. I just came to say how much I appreciate you, sir." He and Mr. Paine shook hands, and Mike turned to Dorcas. "You, too, ma'am. It's been a pleasure to know you all."

Dorcas passed Jenny to her husband and stood up. "We shall miss you sorely. Come here." She stood on tiptoe and kissed his cheek.

"Thank you." Mike hesitated and darted a glance at Lydia.

"Have a safe trip back," she said softly.

Mike bit his lip. "I was hoping I could speak with you privately, but I see you haven't eaten yet. . . ."

"It will keep," Dorcas assured him. "Won't it, Lydia?"

It was suddenly hard to breathe. Lydia swallowed. "I guess it will."

"I won't keep her long. I promise," Mike said, smiling at Mr. and Mrs. Paine. "And I'll behave with perfect propriety."

"Of course you will," said Dorcas.

"Go on, git," said Mr. Paine.

Mike extended his hand and looked into Lydia's eyes. She untied her apron and placed her hand is his.

"There's a full moon rising in the east," Mr. Paine noted.

"Then we shall walk eastward and enjoy the view," Mike said, and Lydia was able to laugh.

When they were away from the wagons and the snorting, shuffling livestock, Mike slowed his steps and halted. Lydia stood beside him in silence, waiting to hear what he would say. He stood staring up at the brilliant moon. His face was tense and his expression very sober.

"I don't want to lose you," he said at last. "Does it have to end here?"

Lydia swallowed hard. *Thank You, Lord,* she cried inwardly, a tumult of praise and joy lifting her spirits beyond all expectation. "What do you suggest?" she whispered.

"Well. . ." He turned and looked down at her. "I was wondering how long your contract is for."

"One year."

"Twelve months?" He reached up and touched her cheek lightly with his fingertips, and Lydia's pulse hammered in her temples. "That's not so long."

She cleared her throat. "One school year, sir."

Mike smiled. "It always helps to be precise."

"Yes."

"Because I make a school year out to be. . .what? Nine months? Ten?"

"I believe school will break after the summer term by July 1 next year. I—I may be mistaken."

"And does your contract forbid you to enter a betrothal during that time?"

"Yes."

He grimaced. "How does the contract feel about suitors in general?"

Lydia smiled. "I'm not to entertain gentleman callers."

"Are you allowed to correspond with. . .say, a lonely noncommissioned officer in the Seventh Dragoons?"

"So far as I know, it's not forbidden."

He nodded and drew a deep breath. "Lydia, my enlistment is up at the end of the year. I've been struggling with what to do after that. I'm thinking I'd like to return to civilian life."

"What would you do?"

"T. R. Barkley wants me to go into the horse business with him, raising horses for the army and the settlers. There's always a shortage of remounts out here."

She nodded. "I think you will succeed. My father raised

horses, and he did well at it. If not for the fire that destroyed his buildings and killed most of his stock, I would probably be quite well off."

"In Hartford, Connecticut," Mike said, and she laughed.

"Yes. Isn't it amazing how God works?"

"Do you believe He bankrupted you to get you out here, Lydia?"

"Perhaps. I only know that having made your acquaintance has made me grateful for this journey in spite of all the hardships."

Mike cleared his throat. "Could you give me an address so that I can send you letters this winter?"

"I'd like that."

"Of course, once the passes are snowed in, there won't be mail for months."

"Then I'll look for a packet of letters in the spring," she said.

He reached to enfold her in his arms, and she didn't hesitate but went to him willingly. He held her close, and Lydia clung to him, slipping her arms around his waist and basking in his warmth and nearness. She felt that he stood between her and the world. For that moment, she couldn't hear, see, smell, or feel anything that wasn't Michael Brown, and it was wonderful. It was the safest, most secure place she had ever known.

"It had to be this way," he whispered, and she raised her face to look up at him. "I asked God to take the memory out of my mind, but He didn't. I just kept remembering that morning in the rocks, when I kissed you. My shoulder hurt like a hot poker was stabbing me, but I forgot all about that when you let me kiss you. If you'd accepted my proposal that day, I would have healed a lot quicker, I'm sure."

"Quit your silliness, Corporal."

Mike's eyes widened. "Is that an order?"

"Yes, sir, it is."

"Fine, then, how's this for gravity?"

He kissed her with all the fire he'd held back on that other occasion, and Lydia melded into his embrace, reveling in the sweetness of the moment. The months ahead would be difficult, but she would not be lonely with this lingering, captivating kiss to remember.

"I feel as if we ought to pray," he said softly when he released her.

"Yes," she whispered.

He folded his arms snugly about her. "Thank You, Father, for this moment. Now show us where to go from here." He buried his face in the crook of her neck. "I love you, Lydia."

"So you've told me," she said, remembering his declaration after the attack by the Sioux.

"Well, that was nothing compared to what I feel now," he said. "You know that if it weren't for the contract, I'd be asking you a certain question right now. When spring comes, as soon as the passes are clear, I'll be back."

"I thought you were going to trade horses with the Nez Perce," she said with a smile.

"I'm coming here first, that's a promise. T. R. and Matt can meet us at old Fort Boise afterward, and we'll jump off from there. If I know T. R.'s wife, Amy, she'll be along, as well. What do you say?"

She laid a hand on his chest. "Careful now. We mustn't—"

"Right. No betrothals yet. I won't stir up any trouble for you with the school board, but when the time comes, you be ready, sweetheart. I intend to be prompt."

As she looked up into his eyes, a deep joy enveloped her. She felt like laughing and singing and shouting at the top of her lungs. She hoped he could read her eager love in her face as she lightly caressed his cheek. Although her words were within the strictest bounds of propriety, the message she conveyed was one of elation. "Thank you, Michael. I shall look forward to it."

epilogue

"I should have stayed in the Army," Mike groaned, pulling on the coat of his new suit.

"Why?" asked his best friend, T. R. Barkley. "So you could get married in your uniform?"

"This suit feels funny."

T. R. shifted his year-old son, Ben, to his other arm. "Aw, that's just because you've spent so many years in uniform. Anything new takes some getting used to."

Mike sighed. He probably would have had nothing but his threadbare old uniform to wear today if Amy Barkley hadn't badgered him into having some new clothes sent out from St. Louis.

"I think you're a little nervous," T. R. said.

Mike ran a hand through his dark hair. "Can't help it. I should have gone to Oregon and fetched her myself."

T. R. shook his head. "It made more sense this way. That mule train of traders was heading out from Oregon City two days after Lydia's school closed. No sense you riding all the way out there to get her, when she could travel with the traders' families. And it gave you time to finish the house."

"True." Mike shoved his hand in his pants pocket and pulled out the gold wedding band he had purchased for Lydia. "Still, when I saw her yesterday, it was like. . ."

"Like you hadn't seen her for most of a year."

"Well, yeah."

T. R. smiled. "She was obviously glad to see you again."

Mike bit his lip, then grinned. "How could she not be?

Oops!" The ring fell to the floor, and he watched it roll across the bare boards.

"Uh-oh," said little Ben.

T. R. laughed. "Uncle Mike dropped the ring, didn't he?"

Mike bent to retrieve it. "Do you think she'll like the house?"

"Relax, Mike. She'll love the house. She'll love the ranch. She'll love living next door to Amy and me. As long as you're there, she'd love anything."

"Yeah." Mike smiled, then thought of another concern. "She's never seen me out of uniform."

His friend shook his head. "It should be a relief to her to see you in civilian clothes, right? No more orders sending you off to who knows where. But, hey, if it will make you feel better, I'll see if Amy can sew a stripe down your pant leg real quick. . ." T. R. watched him expectantly.

Mike laughed.

The door to the barracks opened, and T. R.'s brother, Matt, stepped inside. "The chaplain's ready."

"Great. I don't think I can hold Mike down much longer. Tell the major." T. R. handed his son over to Matt. "And can you hold him during the ceremony?"

"Sure." Matt turned away, and little Ben waved at his father.

Mike exhaled deeply.

"You all right?" T. R. asked.

"I'm fine."

T. R. nodded. "Good. This is the right thing, Mike."

"I know. I'm so thankful God brought her to me. It's just hard to believe it's finally happening. And that she agreed to love, honor, and obey."

"Guess she got that part out of her system, from what you've told me."

"She's headstrong, but she's a wonderful girl, and I wouldn't want her any other way. When you and Amy get to know her better, you'll love her."

"We already love her. She's making you happy, and it's not difficult to see why. She's beautiful, and she's spirited. . .she's got a lot of heart, Mike."

"You make it sound like I'm buying a horse."

T. R. shrugged. "You know what I mean. I'm not one to make flowery speeches. You got a good one. Come on; we should be over at the chapel."

They stepped out of barracks and walked across the parade ground to the new structure of rough boards. Entering by the side door, they were met by the chaplain and guided to stand at the front. The room was filled with cavalrymen, with a sprinkling here and there of wives and other civilians. The band, made up of troopers, was playing Beethoven's "Ode to Joy," but when Mike and T. R. took their places, they began a somewhat shaky rendition of Wagner's "Bridal Chorus."

The men filling the benches in the little chapel quieted as lovely Amy Barkley entered the front door and walked slowly down the aisle to stand near Mike, T. R., and the chaplain. There was a hushed moment; then Amy's father, Major Travis, in his full dress uniform, entered with Lydia on his arm.

Mike's pulse pounded as he stared at his bride. She was breathtaking. Her bouquet of wild flax blossoms brought out the blue of her luminous eyes. It registered in his mind that she was wearing the white dress Amy wore when she married T. R. at Fort Laramie three years earlier, although Lydia was taller than Amy. Mike smiled as he noticed that several inches of delicate lace had been added to the hem of Amy's dress. In her letters during the winter, Lydia had described to him the long evening hours she spent tatting lace. She didn't know what she would use it for, she'd written, but that and correcting her pupils' papers helped keep her mind off how much she missed him.

Their gaze met, and Lydia smiled at him. Mike waited for the moment when Major Travis would hand her over to him, and he could clasp her hand. The future was bright. He had never been so happy, or so certain, he was doing the right thing.

"I love you," he whispered as Lydia reached him. Tears

glistened in her eyes as she joined him and faced the chaplain.

"Dearly beloved. . ."

"I love you," Lydia whispered, so low he could just hear it.

A Letter To Our Readers

Dear Reader:

In order that we might better contribute to your reading enjoyment, we would appreciate your taking a few minutes to respond to the following questions. We welcome your comments and read each form and letter we receive. When completed, please return to the following:

Fiction Editor
Heartsong Presents
PO Box 719
Uhrichsville, Ohio 44683

1. Did you enjoy reading *The Oregan Escort* by Susan Page Davis?
   ❏ Very much! I would like to see more books by this author!
   ❏ Moderately. I would have enjoyed it more if

   _____

   _____

   _____

2. Are you a member of **Heartsong Presents**?   ❏ Yes   ❏ No
   If no, where did you purchase this book? _____

   _____

3. How would you rate, on a scale from 1 (poor) to 5 (superior), the cover design? _____

4. On a scale from 1 (poor) to 10 (superior), please rate the following elements.

   ____ Heroine   ____ Plot
   ____ Hero   ____ Inspirational theme
   ____ Setting   ____ Secondary characters

5. These characters were special because? _____
_____
_____

6. How has this book inspired your life? _____
_____
_____

7. What settings would you like to see covered in future
   Heartsong Presents books? _____
_____
_____

8. What are some inspirational themes you would like to see
   treated in future books? _____
_____
_____

9. Would you be interested in reading other **Heartsong
   Presents** titles?   ❏ Yes   ❏ No

10. Please check your age range:
    ❏ Under 18   ❏ 18-24
    ❏ 25-34   ❏ 35-45
    ❏ 46-55   ❏ Over 55

Name_____
Occupation _____
Address _____
City, State, Zip_____

Hearts♥ng

Presents

Great Inspirational Romance at a Great Price!

Heartsong Presents books are inspirational romances in contemporary and historical settings, designed to give you an enjoyable, spirit-lifting reading experience. You can choose wonderfully written titles from some of today's best authors like Peggy Darty, Sally Laity, DiAnn Mills, Colleen L. Reece, Debra White Smith, and many others.

When ordering quantities less than twelve, above titles are $2.97 each.
Not all titles may be available at time of order.